Chasing I Do

Chasing I Do

The Eastons

MARINA ADAIR

"Adair writes with heart and sizzling heat."
~ JILL SHALVIS, *New Your Times* bestselling author

Text copyright © 2016 Marina Adair
Excerpt from *Promise Me You* copyright © 2016 by Marina Adair

ISBNs: 978-0-9974832-0-8

Cover photograph by Devi Pride of Devi Pride Photography
http://www.devipridephotography.com/
Headshot by Tosh Tanaka

To my dear friend and Kappa Sigma Hottie sister,
Catherine Bybee. Thank you for the support,
the laughs, and the friendship.
I treasure you!

Newsletter

Get the inside scoop on upcoming appearances, giveaways, book releases, and all things Marina Adair delivered right to your inbox! Don't wait, sign up today and join the club!

Sign Me Up!

XOXO,

Marina Adair

Chapter One

Darcy Kincaid had dreamed about this day since she was six and uncovered her mother's stash of *Southern Wedding* magazines in the basement. After a lifetime of planning, hand picking two thousand of the palest of pink peonies, and her entire life savings, she was about to pull off, what she believed to be, the most romantic I Do in history. The sun was high, the sky was crystal blue, and a gentle June breeze carried the scent of the nearby primrose blooms and ever after.

Today was the perfect day to be married, and the rose garden at Belle Mont House was the ideal backdrop. And Darcy wasn't about to let a tail-chasing wedding crasher ruin her moment. No matter how charming.

Not this time.

"Nuzzling the bride's pillows before the wedding will only get you escorted out," Darcy said to the four legged powderpuff in matching pink booties and hair bow.

The dog, who was more runway than runaway, dropped down low in the grass, eyes big black circles of excitement, tail wagging with delight— her jewel-encrusted collar winking in the sunlight.

Darcy squinted, but could only make out the first word, "Fancy."

The little dog's ears perked up and her tail went wild.

"Such a pretty name," Darcy cooed, taking a cautious step forward. "I'm Darcy, it's nice to meet you. I'm going to come a little closer so I can get a better look at your collar and find your mamma's number. Is that okay?"

With a playful snort, the animal's entire body began to wiggle, as if so excited by the idea of making a friend she couldn't contain herself. Darcy reached out to ruffle her ears and Fancy, confusing Darcy's movement for *time to play,* snatched up the pillow—and gave it a good shake.

"No!" Darcy cried, halting in her tracks while little bits of stuffing leached into the air, causing perspiration to bead on her forehead.

Fancy, on the other hand, wasn't worried in the slightest. Nope, she gave another rambunctious whip of the head before jumping up and down with the pillow as if this were all fun and games.

Sadly, this situation was about as close to fun and games as natural child birthing. Not only was the vintage silk pillow, a family heirloom passed down from the bride's great-grandmother, in danger of becoming a chew-toy—but the bride's ring was swinging dangerously from the aged ribbon.

And this wasn't just any bride. Candice Covington was the former Miss Oregon, a Portland mover and shaker, and the first bride to be wed at the newly renovated Belle Mont House. Candice was already in the bridal suite, her beloved in the tower room, and two-hundred of their closest friends and family were set to start arriving in just over an hour—and the dog looked content to nuzzle the pillow all afternoon.

With its teeth.

"Stop," she said, in her most authoritative tone, putting her hand out.

To Darcy's surprise, the dog stopped. Her snout going into hyper-sniffer mode, she dropped the pillow to the grass and rose up to smell the air. Seemed Fancy had caught the scent of the prosciutto wrapped figs sitting on a chair that Darcy had been tasting, and stood up on her hind legs, then walked around in three perfect circles.

"Someone's got moves," she said. "Not bad, but mine are better."

A decade of planning events for Portland's pickiest clients and four years in the trenches as a single mother had taught Darcy the art of positive redirection. She'd lasted through potty training, teething, *and* the chicken pox. This stubborn ball of fluff didn't stand a chance.

Eying the flower arrangement on the closest table, Darcy grabbed a decorative stick and gave it a little shake. "Want to play with the stick for a while?" The dog sat, eyes wide, head cocked to the side in an explosion of cuteness. "We can switch toys before you destroy the pillow, okay?"

"*Yip!*"

Tail up like a heat-seeking radar, the dog hit the fetch-and-retrieve position, pointing her nose toward one of the open fields.

"Ready?" Darcy wiggled the stick again for show. "Go get 'em."

The stick flew through the air, going as far in the opposite direction as it could. Darcy released a sigh of relief when it cleared the fountain and landed in the middle of the field.

A low growl sounded, followed by a blur of white fur that bolted past.

Those little legs working for the prize. A position Darcy could relate to.

Located in the prestigious West Hills, Belle Mont House was three stories of Portland history with extensive manicured gardens, six bedrooms, a grand salon, and captivating views of the city and Mount Hood—all of which needed to be meticulously cared for. And Darcy was the sole caretaker.

She had driven by the old property a thousand times over the years. But hadn't really recognized its potential until after her world had fallen apart, and a heartbreaking betrayal had left her life in tatters—much like the foundation of this forgotten house. Unable to watch something so beautiful and full of history crumble, she'd saved it from demolition, then spent every penny and waking moment renovating it back to its original grandeur. In return, Belle Mont had given her something even more precious—a future for her and her daughter.

Today marked Belle Mont's first day in operation as the year's "Most Romantic" wedding destination in the Pacific Northwest, and Darcy as it's planner extraordinaire—according to the editor at *Wedding Magazine*, who'd left a message earlier about sending a high-profile couple to check out the location.

A couple so hush-hush, the editor refused to give the name for fear that the press would show. But if they decided that Belle Mont was their dream wedding venue, and Darcy could accommodate them with the last Sunday in July, the only date that worked around the couple's hectic schedule, then Belle Mont would land a huge spread in the August issue.

The endorsement alone was enough to make her say yes on the spot. Not to mention the profit for hosting such a lavish event would go a long way toward helping pay back all of the money she'd invested into the renovation—and secure her future in Portland.

A future which now resided in the jaws of a dog that could fit in her pocket.

Fancy snatched the stick and darted across the lawn toward the twinkle lit and peony covered gazebo in record time—all with the pillow still in its jowls.

"Hey," she called out. "We had a deal!"

The dogs tail went up as if flipping the bird at their deal, before she ran beneath a row of chairs and struck a different kind of pose all together. A move that showed enough doggie bits to prove that under that pink bling, Fancy was all male. And about to shit all over Candice's perfect day.

A situation Darcy knew all too well.

"Had I known you had a stupid stick down there, I wouldn't have bothered trying to reason with you."

In Darcy's experience, men loved the forbidden, almost as much as they loved their stick. So she fumbled with her skirt, pulling it above her thighs, and gave chase.

Fancy took off, and man, those toothpick legs could fly. Ears flapping behind him, butt moving like lightning bugs in a jar, the pooch headed straight for the rose garden, which lay directly across from the aisle runner that had CANDICE AND CARTER spelled out in the palest of pink peony petals.

"Not the runner," she cried, only to watch in horror as Fancy raced up the center of the white pillowed Egyptian cotton, his legs pumping with the speed and grace of a cheetah in the wild, leaving a few dozen miniature muddy paw prints and a tornado of petals in his wake.

"No no no," she called out. "Not the rose garden."

Terrified of the damage he could do to the roses, and the pillow, she picked up the pace and rounded the white iron fencing, gravel sliding under heels as she burst through the gate and snatched the pillow right before the Fancy dove his fancy ass—and Candice's ring—into the fountain.

"Got it," she yelled, but the celebration quickly faded as her momentum carried her forward—and right into the stone cherub boy's watering hole.

"Oh God, no!" Darcy yelped, as water exploded around her.

Having landed ass first, she felt the cold wetness seep through her silk skirt and slosh into her shoes. Her brand new designer shoes she'd found at a consignment store and purchased special for today. "Please, no."

She clawed the edge of the fountain and pulled, mentally willing herself out of the fountain—but she couldn't gain any positive momentum. No matter how hard she tried, she just couldn't pull herself out.

Refusing to give up, she looked around for Fancy, hoping to either send him to find help, or pull him in with her. But he'd vanished, right before the wedding, leaving her waist deep in his mess.

The situation was so painfully familiar, Darcy wanted to cry. Then devour the entire wedding cake in one sitting.

"Are you okay?" a husky voice asked from above.

"Thank God you're here," she said, pushing her hair out of her face and looking up, expecting to find one of her kitchen staff.

But instead of a clip-on tie with a comb over, Darcy's unexpected hero looked like an underwear model in a dark blue button-up and a pair of slacks that fit him to perfection. And his arms—*oh my, those arms*—were impressive, perfect for helping a lady in need.

Although Darcy had worked hard to not be reliant on others—a lifetime of letdowns could do that to a girl—she knew that sometimes it was okay to take an offered hand. And those hands were big and solid and—*whoa*—reaching forward to wrap around her hips and easily lift her out.

Her feet hit the floor and she did her best to wring out her shirt. "I'm sorry if I'm getting you all wet."

"You never have to apologize to a man for getting him wet," he chuckled, and Darcy, realizing how *that* had come out, went to move, but his arms tightened, stilling her. "Make sure you're okay first. You were moving pretty fast when you dove in."

Not as fast as her heart was racing.

Closing her eyes, Darcy took stock. Her chest tingled, her head was light, and a wave of delicious thrill jumpstarted parts she'd long believed dead. In fact, she was as far from fine as a woman who had sworn off men could get.

"I'm good. Thank you," she lied, trying to gain some distance without falling back in the fountain, which was not an easy task. He was so big, he filled the space, leaving nowhere for her to go. She brushed off her elbows, which were scraped up, but she'd live, then started to straighten when a big hand appeared. Candice's ring resting in its palm.

"I believe you lost this."

"Thank you," she whispered, a wave of relief washing over her. "You have no idea how…"

Darcy looked up, and the words died on her lips and dropped to the pit of her stomach, where they expanded and churned until—

Oh God, she couldn't breathe.

Her unexpected hero wore slacks and tie fit for wall street, a leather jacket that added a touch of bad boy to the businessman, and a pair of electric blue eyes that she'd recognize anywhere. They'd always reminded her of a calm, crystal clear lake. Today they were tempestuous, like an angry summer storm.

The change wasn't a surprise given the last time they'd seen each other. But the deep ache of longing it brought on was.

"Gage," she breathed, her heart pounding so loudly she was certain he could hear it thumping in her chest.

It was the first time she'd seen him since the funeral, a thought that brought back a dozen others—some sad, some of the best moments of her life, but all of them a painful reminder of what had been lost.

"Hey, Pink," he said in a tone that implied had he known it was her he would have let her drowned.

She swallowed back the disappointment, hoping he didn't notice that she was shaking. "What are you doing here?"

"It looks like I'm helping you find your wedding ring." He took her hand in his and slid the ring on her finger. The sensation was so overwhelming she jerked back.

Gage Easton was over six-feet of solid muscle and swagger. He was also sweet and kind and, at one time, one of the few people she thought she'd always be able to count on. If things had gone how Darcy had dreamed, he would have made for one heck of a brother-in-law.

An even better uncle.

A swift shot of guilt mixed with the swelling panic in her throat, her reckless secret pressing down until she was choking. But Darcy swallowed it back, and refused to shoulder all of the blame.

Life was filled with hard choices. While Gage's twin had chosen to be unfaithful, Darcy had chosen their daughter's happiness.

She would always choose Kylie.

Gage looked at her bare feet then aimed that intense gaze her way. "I would have thought that after jilting Kyle like you did, you'd have started wearing running shoes to these kinds of events."

Although Gage had a big heart, he was still an Easton. And when someone messed with one brother, they messed with the whole clan. The only way to survive was hide your fear and never stand down.

Shoulders back, chest slightly puffed, Darcy made her body appear bigger, the way she had when she'd been a young girl and encountered a stranger at her breakfast table. She'd walk into the kitchen and pretend she was big and strong—someone not to be messed with.

Her mother had a thing for rot-gut whisky and bottom-shelf men—and made a habit of bringing both home. Sometimes they stayed the night, sometimes they stayed the year, but Darcy never knew who—or what—she'd encounter in the one place that should have felt safe.

But this was her home now, and she'd do whatever was necessary to protect it.

"After five years, I would have hoped you'd realize your family weren't the only ones who were hurting," she said. "I may have walked out on your brother, but I wasn't the one who let him drive that night."

Gage Easton felt the truth of that statement hit hard, the power of it nearly taking him out at the knees. Darcy wasn't a confrontational person by nature, but she knew how to stand her ground. No doubt a trait she'd picked up from dealing with his family.

He hadn't seen her since the funeral. Nobody had. Not that he'd blamed her. His family had still been reeling from the aftermath of the wedding that never happened, when tragedy struck again, tearing a chasm between Darcy and the Eastons that could never be fixed. His brother, Kyle, was gone, and with the overwhelming and sudden grief that had been thrust upon his family, most especially his mom, a lot of the blame had been unfairly placed upon Darcy.

There were so many times he wanted to reach out, make sure she was okay, but he'd spent the majority of their relationship keeping his distance, certain that no good could come from letting himself get too close. And he wasn't looking to test his theory.

Not today.

"Are you okay?" he asked, waving a hand to her elbows, which were scraped and he was certain smarting.

"Nothing that won't heal," she said, and he knew she wasn't talking about the gravel burn. "I just have to change my skirt and shoes."

"You might want to change the top while you're at it." He grinned. "Not that I mind the view, but it might cause some heart problems with the older guests."

Darcy's gaze dropped to her shirt and the two beautiful buds peeking through the translucent fabric, and she gasped. Hell, Gage was in his prime and her top was causing some serious gasping and heart palpitations on his end.

"Don't worry, I didn't peek. Much." He leaned in and whispered, "Although, if you know you're going to take a swim, you might just consider skinny dipping. You'd get the same effect, only you wouldn't have to hang-dry your lace bra and panties."

"You can't see my panties."

No, he couldn't, but she didn't need to know that. The narrowed eyes and pursed lips were enough to tell him that she was ticked just thinking about him seeing her panties. And that was a far better state than the tears that had been threatening a moment ago.

"Look," she said pointedly, crossing her arms over her chest, which did nothing—except pull the fabric tighter. "I'm grateful that you found the ring and helped me out of the fountain, and I have no clue as to why you're here," her tone said she didn't care to find out either, "but I need you to leave."

"Don't worry," he said. "I didn't come to ruin your big day. I'll get out of your way as soon as my meeting is over." And he found the abomination in bows he was stuck dog sitting.

"Oh, it's not *my* big day," she clarified. "I'm the planner for the wedding that is supposed to start in less than an hour."

He looked at her outfit, while although cream and dripping, it wasn't bridal attire. The skirt, the buttoned silk top, even her hair said professionally elegant. Not bride to be.

A heaviness that he didn't even notice he'd taken on lifted at her admission, and he wanted to kick himself. She wasn't getting married? So what? It didn't matter. Kyle was gone, Gage was still struggling to make peace with things, and Darcy would always be off limits.

No matter how great she still looked. Even scratched up and sweaty, she was as gorgeous as ever.

"Well, if you'll just direct me to the manager's office," he asked. "I'm late and don't want to keep him waiting."

She looked at her watch and froze, an expression of resignation washing over her.

"Actually, you're early," she said, so full of dread he felt sweat bead on his forehead. She stuck out her hand. "Darcy Kincaid, owner and exclusive planner for Belle Mont House. I believe the editor from *Wedding Magazine* said you'd be dropping by tomorrow."

Chapter Two

"Can you define exclusive for me?" Gage asked, not sure if he was going to laugh or lose his shit. Both were distinct possibilities, and he knew with complete certainty that he was screwed.

"It means I am the only person allowed to design, plan, or oversee events at Belle Mont House," she said, her eyes full of fire, her attitude dialed to untouchable.

Which in no way explained why his fingers itched to reach out. Sure, he liked fire and attitude on his women. He'd always especially liked it on this particular woman. But after five years of no contact and a boatload of disappointment—on both sides—he'd assumed he'd gotten past the attraction.

She'd made her choice, and he'd made peace with it.

"And what if my client wants someone else to plan the event?"

"Then they need to find a new venue. I have a list of recommendations in the office," she said, ever so helpful. "Just let me know who your client is and I'll have my assistant send it over."

She handed him a card, which she pulled from who knows where. The point was, she stepped forward to give it to him, so close he could see the sun dance in her eyes, and he caught a whiff of something floral and—*Jesus help him*—sexy.

"I'm not at liberty to say who the event is for until we have nondisclosure agreements signed," he said, and she rolled her eyes. Right, lame excuse, but he knew the second she heard who his client was, any bargaining chip he held would be voided. "What can I do to make you feel comfortable entertaining the idea of bringing in someone else to plan the wedding?"

"Nothing."

The way she said it, with a bravado that was too big to be real, told him that she wasn't as rigid as she was letting on. As an agent for some of the world's top musicians and sports stars, Gage had negotiated enough deals to know that everyone had a price—it wasn't always money, although money was the easiest to leverage.

But nothing with him and Darcy had ever been easy.

"Look, they don't want another venue, they want Belle Mont House. My client's fiancée is set on having it here." Only because she'd heard some European princess who was loosely related to Grace Kelley had been married there once upon time. "But he will only agree to it if you ensure that it won't turn into a media frenzy. Can you guarantee that?"

Gage watched the way those beautiful eyes darted around the grounds. He knew what she was seeing. Besides the assistant she'd mentioned, there were only a few hired servers and wait staff walking around, and if her wedding was to start in an hour, he doubted she had more coming. Bottom line: she didn't have a staff large enough to handle a high-profile event. Let alone one that could easily become a media circus. And she knew it.

"If security is a concern, I can look into a solution that would satisfy your client's concerns. I'd even be open to using a security company he's used before," she said. "But as far as running the event, I was very upfront with Lana that I would design and plan the wedding."

Shit.

"Lana didn't mention that," he said, referring to the magazine editor he'd spent the last two weeks courting to make this last-minute-wedding happen. A deal that, if it went south, his client would have his ass.

And it wasn't just any client, it was his biggest client. Rhett Easton, prodigy guitarist, front man for one of *Rolling Stone's* bands-to-watch, and one of Gage's older brothers. While Rhett was finishing up the press tour for his band's first album, Gage had been drafted to make sure his upcoming wedding went off without any problems.

Which wouldn't have been a problem if they'd decided to be like every other couple on the planet and give themselves at least a year to plan a wedding.

"How much would it cost for you to look the other way for once and let someone else run the show?" Gage asked.

"I looked the other way once. It didn't work out so well for me," she said, painful silence weighing thick in the air.

"I'm not Kyle," he said quietly.

Even though Kyle and Gage were twins, they couldn't have been more different. Where Kyle was impulsive and outspoken, Gage analyzed every possible outcome and didn't mince words. Kyle loved the flash, and Gage was content to be the guy behind the curtain.

"No, but it doesn't matter, because Kyle will always be there. Every time I think I can move on, start over, he's there."

Anger simmered beneath the surface. "You're blaming him for not being able to move on? It was you moving on so abruptly that landed us all here to begin with."

"You don't think I know that? That every day I don't think, 'If I had just confronted him instead of running, would he still be here?' I know what I did, and I am so sorry for not having the courage to stand up in front of everyone I knew and loved, and say I couldn't go through with the wedding. But things were complicated, Gage. Everything with Kyle was always so complicated, so one sided. The man could fight with a tree stump. Out of everyone, you should know that." She rested a hand on his arm and an intense charge shot though him.

He looked down at her hand and let it stay there, just this once, let the heat of her hand melt through the fabric, slide along his skin, and he imagined what it would feel like to have her touch other places on his body.

"I get why your mom blames me," she said, and his gaze jerked to hers. "But at some point, I figured the emotions would fade and you would see that maybe there was more to the story than me getting cold feet."

Gage wasn't sure what had gone down between Darcy and Kyle, but for as many great things as Kyle had done, he'd also racked up some pretty shitty ones.

When their dad passed away, Kyle took it the hardest. He was so angry at the world he ignored the strength and direction he'd gained from working alongside a man as great as Benjie Easton. He tended to veer off course from time to time and make questionable decisions, but Darcy had a calming strength that grounded him.

"I'm not asking you to forgive me, Gage. I'm just asking you to under-stand," she said. "I've worked too hard to rebuild this house to ever look the other way again."

"Even if you lose what could be the biggest wedding of your career?"

"Your client is looking for a premiere venue with a six-week lead time at the beginning of peak wedding season. There is no other option."

"You and I both know that a spread in *Wedding Magazine* opens up a lot of options."

"It does, but your client signed a deal with *Wedding Magazine*," she said. "They signed it knowing that they'd be working with me. I already gave Lana a verbal agreement, so as far as I am concerned, *your* issues with *me* have nothing to do with this deal. If you don't want to see me, then don't come, but don't you use those big agent," she punctuated the last two words with a finger to his pec, "scare tactics on me, Gage. I've seen you negotiating a multi-million-dollar contract, just like I've seen you begging to the porcelain god for mercy after too many tequila shots. So you don't scare me."

Darcy was good at masking her emotions, but he knew her well enough to see the signs. She was scared of losing this account.

"I'm not trying to scare you, just pointing out the facts," he said. "If my client walks because of your unwillingness to be flexible, do you really think *Wedding Magazine* won't just roll over for the chance to follow him to the next venue?"

He watched her confidence fade and the uncertainty of it all take over as the woman, who'd once looked at him with nothing but warmth and trust, looked up at him with panic and betrayal in those caramel eyes.

"I know you have no reason to help me, Gage. But I can do this. I need to do this wedding," she said quietly. "You know how good I am, and how much I'd bring to this kind of event. Your client won't get the same experience with any other planner. I'm not asking for a handout. I'm just asking for a fair shot."

There was something about the way she looked at him, it was the same look she'd had when she'd confided in him about how hard she'd worked to create a better life than the one she'd been born into, that tugged at his heart. That made him want to give in.

So he glanced up at the sky and took a deep breath, trying like hell to distance himself from the desperation he saw on her face. What it was about the leggy brunette with the sad smile that still got to him? It was her eyes, he decided. Her big, brown, melt-your-soul eyes that he could never ignore.

She was as real as a woman could get. Funny, caring, sexy, and so damn warm it drew people in. Darcy didn't just listen, she took a genuine interest and great care with peoples' dreams—with their lives. Around her, he couldn't help but feel loved.

Which was why her runaway bride moment had come as such a shock. Darcy was honest, loyal, and devoted—right up until the second she walked out on Kyle and shattered his world.

No, she didn't let him drive that night, but Kyle wouldn't have been at a bar shitfaced and spinning off his axis if she'd handled things differently.

So yeah, he'd signed that magazine deal on Rhett's behalf. And, yeah, it was obvious Darcy needed the publicity this would bring, but none of that mattered. It had taken his family five years to get back on track, and he wasn't about to blow that. This time, his mother would see her son walk down the aisle.

Collateral damage or not, Darcy had to go.

"The client is Rhett," he said, and her face went completely pale. "So you being the planner is not an option."

"I was hired to plan an Easton wedding?"

"Yup. Which is why I'll have a list of five of the best planners in the country emailed to you tomorrow. I'll leave it up to you to pick the final one, but, Darcy, if you want this event, it won't be you." Then, before he gave in to the way her eyes misted over, Gage upped his douche factor and hollered, "Fancy, come."

Gage walked through the doors of the historical craft beer bar in downtown, letting loose a string of choice words when he saw three of his five brothers. He knew why they were there. Even knew why they wore amused as shit looks on their faces.

After the day he'd had, Gage wanted nothing more than to go home, shower, and grab a cold beer. Which was ironic, because the day he'd had left the first two as non-options. Only leaving the cold beer still in play.

That was the reason he'd asked his brothers to meet.

Stout was known, not only for its deal making environment, working as the official meeting place for politicians, businessmen, and celebrities, but it was started by their late father. So not only did it feel like a second home, it was the one place the brothers always came when they needed to talk.

And tonight, they had a lot to consider.

Deciding the best course of action was to man-up, take the reaming, then drop the bomb that was sure to wipe those smug looks right off their faces, Gage headed toward the bar. Fancy pranced behind him with his head high and his tail waving proudly, as if he wasn't the pussiest dog known to man.

"You courting a new client around town?" Clay, the youngest and, up until two seconds ago, his favorite brother, wanted to know. He was dressed in his usual sports jersey with a cracked lip and black eye, looking as if he'd been in a bar fight or training hard for the upcoming season—which being an NFL MVP, it could have been either.

"Funny thing about that," Gage said, handing Rhett the leash. "I called Stephanie to see where she wanted to meet for the hand-off, you know, the one I offered to do on the way to my big meeting, because you were at that interview and she couldn't make it to the groomer in time. She explained she was getting her dress fitted in L.A., then thanked me for agreeing to dog sit."

"That was nice of you," Rhett said, picking up the dog and setting him in his lap.

"I'm not dog sitting," Gage clarified. "And how the hell is she supposed to plan a wedding if she's out of state?"

"The woman could organize a hostile takeover of a first world country from her iPhone." Rhett leaned back and folded his hands behind his head, making himself right at home. "The in-person stuff, that's why we have you."

"You don't *have* me. I said I'd pull a favor with the location. Not plan a wedding while dog sitting a glorified rat who likes to tear off people's fingers." He glared at Fancy, who was too busy licking himself to notice. "What's up with that?"

"They must have been wearing R-I-N-G-S," Rhett said.

"Rings?"

Littleshit lunged forward, nearly taking Gage's hand off in the process. "Jesus, what's wrong with that thing?"

"Nothing." Rhett patted the rat's head in praise. "Stephanie paid some fancy dog trainer to the stars to teach him how to carry the rin—" Rhett stopped abruptly when Fancy's eyes went into Cujo mode. "He's our R-I-N-G bearer, so he'll carry *it* down the aisle."

Rhett pointed to his ring finger in case anyone missed what *it* referred to. Then he glanced at Gage's shirt, wrinkled with little muddy paw prints, and grinned. "How did the meeting with the potential client go?"

"He was the NHL's rookie of the year, right?" Owen, the middle brother and the owner of Stout, asked. He reached over the bar to refill the pitcher, sure to ruffle Littleshit's ears in the process. "Tony Carter. He was in here the other night, served him and a couple of his teammates. Nice guy, big tipper."

"But did he seem like a dog lover?" Rhett asked, and all of the brothers burst out laughing. Loud, amused, shit-eating laughter that made Gage want to punch someone in the nuts.

Even Littleshit was laughing. Those lips of his peeled back to give a nice flash of his damn needle teeth. The ones that had done a bang up job of turning his leather car seats into strips of jerky on the ride over.

"Didn't matter," Gage said, taking a seat, sure to elbow Rhett in the process. "Told him my brother was so pussy-whipped that he had a set of matching bows and collar at home that his soon-to-be-wife bought him. Playtime attire, is what I hear they call it."

"Jesus, man," Rhett said, suddenly serious. "That leaks and the press will run with it. I'll never be able to go into a pet store again without someone wondering why I'm buying dog treats."

Fancy never came up in his meeting because he paid the doorman at his building a hundred bucks to watch the rat while he landed a new client. Not that Gage mentioned that to Rhett. He'd gone out of his way to screw with Gage's day, so letting him sweat it out for a bit wouldn't hurt.

His career was on the verge of taking off, everyone knew it, including Rhett, who was working non-stop to make sure nothing hindered him from taking it all the way. From Stout to stadiums was the band's motto. And they were almost there.

So when he asked Gage to fix the problem, Gage wanted to be the guy to fix it. The guy to make all of the shit in their lives disappear. Make it so whenever they saw each other it didn't feel like there was a gaping hole in their world.

But Gage hadn't only felt the void of Kyle these last few years, he'd felt the loss of Darcy as well. And seeing her today, a little battered but determined, had messed with his head. So he'd called his brothers. Josh, the oldest, was out of town on business, but the others had dropped what they were doing and come right over.

"Belle Mont House comes with its own wedding planner." Gage leveled with his brothers. "Darcy bought Belle Mont house a few years back."

"Holy hell," Rhett said, his face the same degree of *what-the-fuckery* that had taken Gage three hours to come to terms with.

"Wait. Kyle's Darcy?" Owen asked.

Gage wanted to point out that she wasn't his anymore; she wasn't any of theirs, but knew that they needed time to process. Hell, he was still processing.

He watched as the reality of Darcy being back in their lives began to sink in. Watched as his brothers' expressions went from dumbfounded to anger, and finally sadness. Gage remembered what Darcy had said earlier, that they weren't the only ones who had lost out, and found himself wondering who she'd leaned on.

"Does Mom know?" Clay asked, bringing Gage back to reality, back to the only person who really mattered.

"If she doesn't, she will," Gage said. "Darcy is adamant that no outside planner can be brought in." Knowing how his mom would react if she learned Darcy owned the house, he didn't blame her. "So, unless Stephanie wants to consider some other options…"

"It isn't just Steph," Rhett said. "Mom was with her when she got the call from *Wedding Magazine*. They've both been clipping out wedding pictures and talking nonstop about it. I haven't seen Mom this excited in years. Hell, she's so excited that we're getting married here instead of LA, she even made a Pinterest board with ideas that she updates hourly."

"What if we offer her an out-of-network vendor fee or something," Owen said. "I do it all the time here when someone wants to book the bar for an event but bring in their own caterer."

"I don't think a few extra grand is going to sway her." After his ill-thought threat, he didn't think anything shy of a public apology from every member of his family would sway her. "Plus, money doesn't motivate her."

"How do you know?" Owen said, crossing his arms in challenge. "She seemed to change her mind the second Kyle's finances took a turn."

Gage never agreed with his family's consensus that Kyle's financial status had a role in her decision to skip the wedding. Darcy was never looking for a hand-out. She was looking for a partner. Someone to love, who would love her back. "I just know."

Rhett studied him long and hard. "If you're so sure that money won't sway her, then how about you?"

"What?"

"Well, you're the one who claims to *know her*." Owen threw up air quotes. "I forgot how close you two used to be before she and Kyle hooked up."

Too close. "No way."

"It's actually not a bad idea. She's always liked you, trusted you," Clay added.

"Not anymore." *Not after today.* "And even if she did, that doesn't mean she'd change her policy. Especially for an Easton wedding."

Jesus, Darcy was right. Saying it aloud made him realize what an impossible situation this was. Them expecting Darcy to agree would be like her asking Rhett to play at her wedding. Worse even, this wasn't just her place of work, it was her home.

"She won't change her mind," he said, confident now in that fact, even if he wasn't okay with it.

"She would change it for you," Rhett said, so serious that apprehension twisted in Gage's stomach. "And if she's worried about the house, tell her I'll bring in my best people."

"What people?" Gage laughed, but it was more of a release of emotion. It had been one hell of a day and he was about at his breaking point. "You mean your roadies?"

"No, I mean I will have Steph call the company that catered for Oprah when she interviewed her. I will provide background checks on every employee who walks on that property. And I will give every media outlet exclusive pictures from the wedding when it's over. It might even land her a cover." Rhett sounded so serious that Gage began to believe that it might work. "And I will personally vouch for everyone invited, as long as Stephanie gets her dream wedding and Mom gets to see us walk down the aisle without a reminder of Kyle hanging over her head."

"And will you personally apologize for what happened at the funeral?" Gage asked, ignoring the shocked looks on his brothers' faces.

He'd worked hard to do the right thing, to avoid situations where he treated others unfairly. After seeing the absolute conviction in Darcy's eyes when she said there was more to the story, Gage began to question everything he'd assumed to be just.

Including how his family had treated her after the wedding day.

"Are we all going to apologize? Because, let's face it, there is no way she'd feel comfortable letting Mom on the property after the fall-out they had."

And by fall-out, he meant his mom having Darcy arrested for trying to get her stuff out of Kyle's apartment, then accusing her in the news for the death of her son.

"When did you become Debbie Downer?" Rhett asked.

Gage had no idea. He was the guy with the plan, the brother who could find an upside to any problem.

Years of negotiating multi-million dollar contracts for some of the biggest egos in sports and music had taught Gage that most life decisions were driven by emotional needs. People didn't haggle over an extra half-percent—they were searching for validation. The key to closing a deal was pinpointing what that meant to each person, then delivering it in a way that both sides felt as if they'd been heard.

Darcy didn't want money, and she didn't give in to threats. All she wanted was an honest conversation. And his brothers were right, the only one who could give her that was him.

Chapter Three

The wedding was in full swing and already deemed a success.

So why couldn't Darcy pull herself out of the tailspin that Gage had started? He'd always had the ability to get straight to the heart of the matter, and today was no exception. Only this time, her heart hadn't seemed to matter to him.

Which was okay.

She herself had made a lot of decisions in recent years where his best interests weren't a factor. Something she'd thought about non-stop since she told him to take his offer and his dog somewhere else.

Although, after a quick google search, she'd learned it wasn't his dog, but it belonged to one of his clients. Stephanie Stone, to be exact. One of the most recognized names on the internet, a mover and shaker in the national media, and soon to be renamed Stephanie Easton.

Hosting her wedding would be huge for Darcy—and Belle Mont House. And even though passing on the opportunity had been a smart move, it had left an unsettled feeling that was too intense to ignore. Which was why Darcy needed some perspective.

Behind her, the sweeping music swelled as couples spun around the dancefloor in tuxedoes and elegant ball gowns, love and forever thick in the summer air. While above her, a million or so white lights twinkled, turning the rose garden and bubbling brook trail into a romantic paradise. But to Darcy, the most perfect part of the night was standing on the grass in front of the guest cottage, twirling under the stars.

Darcy stopped at the edge of the foot bridge that separated the main property from her cottage, her heart swelling with love as she watched her two-foot-tall ballerina lead a neighbor boy around the lawn. Dressed in pink feetie-pajamas with little puppies scattered down the front, a pair of Darcy's pumps, and a veil someone left in the bridal suite decades ago, was the reminder she needed.

Darcy's reason.

"You didn't start without me, did you?" Darcy asked.

Kylie stopped dancing and turned around. The moment she saw Darcy her smile went radiant, and she let out a giggle that had the power to change the world.

"Mommy," she said, clapping her hands and jumping up and down, the heels of the borrowed pumps making little divots in the moist lawn. "Look, Sammy, it's my mommy. Mommy, did you see us twirling?"

"I sure did."

"I told her I should be twirling her 'cuz I'm a boy, but she keeps twirling me," Sam said, sounding put out.

Kylie jabbed her little fists into her hips and said, "It's only 'cuz I know how to do it better. When you twirl me, you step on my veil."

And even though Sam was two years older, a foot taller, and hated playing princess dance party, he always seemed content to indulge Kylie. Even when he'd rather be playing video games. And it was clear by the sleepy eyes, he'd been playing the doting partner for a little while.

"Well, that was very nice of you to play Kylie's game with her, Sam." Darcy looked at her daughter, prompting, "Wasn't it Kylie?"

"Uh huh," Kylie said. Then, hands clasped in front of her, she started twisting side to side. "Thanks, Sammy," she sang.

Sensing his exit had finally arrived, Sam grunted, then ran inside the house, shouting something about video game time as he passed his mom.

"Ten minutes, then it's time to get ready for bed," Jillian called back with a smile.

Jillian Conner was the exclusive cake designer for Belle Mont. The two had met a few years back in Mommy & Me. But it wasn't until Jillian's husband filed for divorce, and she started baking sweets in her home to supplement her income, that the two bonded. Now, they were close friends, supporting each other through the trials and limitations that came with single-motherhood.

Swapping babysitting hours, craft ideas, and sharing in the joy that came with kids.

"I think Sam's dance card was full," Jillian chuckled from the rocking chair on the front porch. She wore ballet flats, khaki capris, and a white top with a bright yellow gauzy scarf twisted into some complicated knot around her neck. Her short chestnut hair was layered and effortlessly sexy. Anyone else might run the risk of looking like a soccer mom, but only someone with Jillian's grace could pull off holly-homemaker with class.

"I think it's because the carriage is about ready to turn into a pumpkin." Darcy made her way toward the lawn to pick up her daughter. "Are you going to turn into a mouse?"

"Not a mouse, a dog!"

"Well, then I'd better get you to bed before you start barking at me," she said, sending Kylie into an eruption of giggles that filled the night—and Darcy's chest.

It was crazy how one giggle, one little smile could make all of the problems that had seemed so insurmountable moments ago vanish.

Kylie wasn't just her daughter. She was her everything.

They may be a small family, but their love was mighty. Darcy carried enough for two parents—enough to last a lifetime. The day she'd discovered she was pregnant, she'd made a promise, to herself and to her baby, that they would live a life built on happiness, honesty, and never-ending love.

Three things Darcy never had much of growing up.

She had sacrificed a lot to hold true to that promise, but when she heard her daughter's joyous laughter float up into the night sky, she knew it was worth every hardship.

Sometimes, it seemed as if both of their lives had begun the day Kylie was born. Darcy, who had been on her own for most of her life, found herself alone once again after Kyle's death. But then Kylie came along, and suddenly emotions and this tangible connection that Darcy had struggled for years to find came bubbling to the surface with such force they infused every corner of her life.

A life, she thought, taking in the small guest cottage they called home, that she was proud of.

"Let's get washed up for bed," Darcy said.

"But they're playing the chicken dance. I do the chicken good. Look." Kylie tucked her arms in, like wings, and flapped for her life.

"You do, but it's way past bedtime." Darcy set her daughter on her feet and led them to the porch. "Say goodnight to Auntie Jillian."

"But they haven't cut the cake." Kylie's lower lip quivered in a way that made saying no hard. "And it's my favorite kind."

"And what kind would that be?" Darcy asked, her eyes on Jillian in question, because she'd been so busy doing damage control, she wasn't even sure what kind of cake the bride had ordered.

"The iced kind," Jillian said, and Kylie's head bobbled in agreement.

"Then I will bring you a slice for tomorrow." Before her daughter could come up with yet another reason to prolong bedtime, Darcy added, "If you are a good girl and go to bed for me."

Quivering stopped and Kylie gave Jillian a big smack to the lips. "Night, Auntie."

"Night, sugar," Jillian said. "Make sure Sam is getting ready too."

"Sammy," Kylie called, dragging out his name from two to nine syllables. "It's bed time."

Darcy waited until she heard heels clacking hard enough against the wood floors to leave marks, then let out a breath. "Thanks for staying the night. You're a lifesaver."

"My pleasure. Sam needed a playdate that didn't involve videogames, plastic guns, or tackle."

"Tackle football?"

"No, just tackle." Jillian shrugged. "Boys, they're a different breed."

Didn't she know it.

Darcy took a seat in the rocking chair next to her friend, and watched the people across the lake dance and hug and mingle, as if nothing could come between them. As if the only emotion in that moment was hopeful joy.

It was why Darcy loved weddings so much. They were the day when everything was perfect, and everyone was connected through love.

"I heard you had a problem with the aisle runner earlier," Jillian said.

"I called the nursery and replaced the runner with a blanket of pink and cream petals." It had cost her a small fortune, and she was sure to take a loss on the flowers, but the bride had been thrilled. "I found out who the celebrity wedding was for."

"Oh. My God." Jillian's brows shot up. "Who is it?"

"I'm not supposed to say, the magazine swore me to confidentiality."

"Only so that they could have one of their interns unintentionally spill the news at the right moment, so it will start a media frenzy to get everyone talking about the wedding of the year. A million readers anxiously awaiting the exclusive photos in their magazine." Jillian motioned with her hand to bring it. "Let me be the insider who spills."

"I can't say."

"It's one of the Hemsworth brothers, isn't it?" Darcy shook her head and Jillian squealed. "It's Scott Eastwood. Please tell me it's Scott Eastwood?"

"No." Darcy bit her lower lip. "It's Rhett Easton."

Shock filled her friend's face, followed by sympathy. "Oh, honey, Kyle's brother? What are the odds of that happening?"

"One in a billion." She slumped down in her chair. "I keep looking for the hidden cameras, because this has to be some cruel joke. There is no way that I finally get the opportunity to secure mine and Kylie's future, and it all comes down to an Easton." A bad taste formed in her mouth. "Karma can suck it."

"What did he say? Did he smell like wall-banging sex? I heard he's into wall sex. Which makes sense, the man is too sexy to want to do it someplace ordinary like a bed. Oh!" Jillian clapped. "Please tell me be brought his fiancée? I always wondered if her boobs were real." Jillian looked down at her own boobs and cupped them. "They have to be fake, they defy gravity."

"Rhett didn't come. He sent his brother Gage."

"Oh no," Jillian said, placing a hand over Darcy's, because she knew the whole story, knew that getting sucker punched by Gage would hurt the most.

"He seemed as surprised to find me here as I was him. So at least being blindsided wasn't some sick joke," she said in a voice that she hoped came off as nonchalant. She left out the part that she'd flirted with him a little before she'd realized who it was. "Needless to say, it didn't go well."

"He canceled the wedding?" Jillian said fiercely. "What a jerk."

"No, I canceled it." And *yes*, he'd been a jerk.

"What? Why? He's marrying Stephanie Stone. The exposure alone would be amazing for you." Jillian's voice became velvet steel. "Don't let Kyle ruin this moment for you, not when that income could make all the difference in your career. You've built something amazing here that deserves to host amazing weddings."

That was the only reason Darcy had even considered calling him back. This wasn't just about her and Kylie anymore, she now had fifteen employees and small business owners counting on her to make this venue a success. Not to mention a loan from the bank that needed to be paid back.

"I can't do an Easton wedding here. It would be uncomfortable and awkward, and just thinking about seeing Margo makes me nauseous." The throbbing in her head returned. "I've worked so hard to give Kylie a happy and safe place to grow up. I won't risk that for just one wedding."

"What if you are risking something even bigger?" Jillian asked gently. "Wouldn't it be nice to have someone else to count on? Someone else who loves Kylie as much as you do? Jerry might be a cheating jerk with a bad case of slippery dick syndrome, but Sam lights up every time his dad picks him up for their weekends."

Darcy swallowed hard. She knew what it was like to grow up in a single parent household. Her earliest memories were of having dry cereal for dinner because it was all that was in the house, and tucking herself in at night because her mom was working—or out at the bars spending her paycheck.

Between holding down two jobs and looking for the next man to latch onto, Darcy's mom was usually so tired, something had to take a back seat. Sadly, it was often Darcy.

Which was why Darcy went into parenthood determined to be an amazing mom. Having a family was what she'd always wanted. More than anything. She couldn't imagine a life without Kylie.

But did Kylie wonder what a life with a dad might be like? Darcy had. Not having a father had left a giant hole in her childhood, and she was determined that Kylie would always have enough.

Enough food. Enough clothes. Enough love.

"They don't want me," she admitted, hating how bad it still burned. "They want to bring in an outside planner, and you know how temperamental the house is. You have to bang the AC just to get it started, and if someone doesn't jiggle the upstairs toilet handle, it will fill up the septic tank."

Dead silence. "The AC and a toilet is the reason you turned down a wedding that could get you close to breaking even on this place?"

"Yes," Darcy lied.

Jillian shot her a skeptical look, but played along. "Well, then if that is your only concern, counter their offer. Tell Gage you need a bigger deposit, or that you are a non-negotiable part of the deal. Belle Mont House isn't the magic ingredient to captivating romance, you are, so let them know that. This is your house and your dream. Don't miss out because of something some guy from your past did. He's taken enough from you and Kylie."

"Thanks," Darcy said, wiping the emotion forming in the corner of her eyes away. "I needed to hear that."

"Mom-my," Kylie's voice came from down the hall. "I'm rea-dy."

Darcy gave her friend a long hug. Drying her eyes, she walked into the house and into Kylie's bedroom. Painted a light blue with green grass, a dog mural, and paw print trim, it was the only room that had been remodeled in the cottage. And sitting on the bed with a doghouse bedframe was her daughter, cuddled up with her favorite stuffed animal.

"Lights out time." Darcy reached for the switch.

"But we haven't played High-Low yet," Kylie said, referring to the game they played every night at the dinner table. "And we always play High-Low."

Darcy looked at her watch and sighed. She needed to get back to the wedding. She'd already been gone longer than expected. But her daughter needed a few more minutes of her attention, and Darcy needed one more hug, so she sat on the corner of the mattress. "Okay, high first."

"Auntie Jillian took us to the harbor to see the sea lion babies, and after she bought us an ice cream," Kylie said with a sneaky smile. "A double scoop too, for big girls. And it had gumballs in it that turned my tongue colors." Her tongue peeked out, and even though it was back to pink, Darcy covered her heart with her hand, and gasped.

"I can see that. It matches your pajamas," Darcy said, and Kylie beamed. "Now low?"

"She made broccoli with dinner and I had to eat the whole plate full." Kylie's face puckered like she'd sucked on lemon, then tugged her stuffed dog toward her.

"A whole plate full, huh?" Darcy teased, knowing Jillian put four pieces of broccoli on her plate—one for every year old Kylie was. "That is pretty awful."

"Your turn."

"Easy. Watching you twirl." She tapped Kylie's nose, which crinkled at the touch. "The worst part? That's harder. Hmmmm…"

The whom was easy. Gage. Their meeting had been so disappointing she still felt the ache in her chest. Now, deciding which part of the impromptu meet was the most disappointing was the part that had Darcy waffling.

The cold way he'd looked at her earlier had reminded her of how she felt right after Kyle died. Scared, alone, unwanted. And just when she though it couldn't get any worse, he'd dropped that threat on her in a calculated move that was so reminiscent of Kyle in their last few months together, she felt as if she were reliving the heartache all over.

It made her question if she'd gotten everything wrong. If her judgement was so incredibly bad when it came to men that she'd, once again, made a hero out of a self-centered jerk. Not that she would tell Kylie that, but she wouldn't lie either.

"I ran into an old friend and it left me feeling sad," Darcy finally said.

"Oh," Kylie said, her little face soft with concern. "Because you miss them?"

"Yeah, honey." She did miss Gage. Missed their talks, their inside jokes, the way he'd tell her everything would work out.

Nothing had turned out the way they'd expected. But it had turned out exactly how it was supposed to. And even though Darcy had gone through hell to get to where she was, she wouldn't trade one second of her life with Kylie.

"I miss how things used to be," she said. "But I love how things are now. I love you, honey."

"Love you too, Mommy."

Kylie laid back and immediately closed her eyes, feigning sleep. She was so in character, she even let Darcy pull the blankets taut and tuck them snuggly around Kylie's petite frame.

The stuffed dog cuddled beside her daughter caught Darcy's eye, and she looked at the smug little face and smiled. Between all of the drama with Gage and the wedding, she'd completely forgotten about Fancy. "Guess who crashed the wedding today?"

The only answer she got was a fake snore.

"Oh my, she's already asleep," Darcy said to no one in particular. Kylie cracked a smile, but didn't open her eyes.

"Well, I guess I'll just have to tell her tomorrow about the dog that visited Belle Mont House." Darcy stood and clicked off the bedside lamp. Kylie still didn't move. "It was a miniature white Pomeranian named Fancy."

"A Pomeranian?" Kylie bolted straight up and clicked back on the light. "Like Sassy?"

"Yup. Fancy had on pink bows and collar. And you know what else?" Darcy leaned down to whisper, "Fancy was a boy."

Fingers over her mouth, eyes bulging like she'd just learned a national secret, Kylie released a breathy giggle. "But he's got a girl name."

"I know. Isn't that weird?"

Kylie thought about that, then shook her head. "You're taking me to the daddy daughter picnic and that's not weird. Unless." She sucked in a horrified breath. "Are you gonna dress like a boy?"

"Only if I can pretend to be Mr. Sims down at the post office." Darcy furrowed her brow and formed her lips into a stern look of disapproval, then in a Mr. Sims-esque voice, said, "Little girls who don't go to sleep don't get cake."

"For breakfast?"

Tomorrow was Saturday and every kid needed to have cake for breakfast at least once in their life. For this little girl, it was a weekly occasion, but Kylie always acted as if it were the first time. After her day, Darcy might even be open to a Saturday Cake Buffett. "Sure, why not."

"Day old cake is better than right out of the oven cake," Kylie said dreamily, then laid back down.

With one last kiss, because Darcy could never get enough, she turned off the light and watched Kylie close her eyes.

She wondered if there would ever come a time when Kylie would think it was weird that her mom went to everything—including father only events. That she'd one day notice the lack of male presence in her life.

If things had gone differently, her daughter would have had a really great uncle to look up to in Gage. Five great uncles who would pamper and protect her with the fierce Easton love. It made her question her decision to keep them at a distance all these years. Brought back doubts that maybe she wasn't enough for Kylie.

She could love her with everything she had to give, but in the end, would it be the same as being surrounded by a family full of love?

Then there was Margo Easton, and the reign of terror that woman had brought down on Darcy.

Humiliation rolled in her stomach at the memory of being arrested in her own home. The cold handcuffs, the judgmental neighbors, the place she'd worked so hard to make safe—it was all destroyed in that moment. And brought Darcy back to her childhood—to a time when her home was a revolving door, and visits to the police station weren't a school sponsored field trip.

Margo knew, *knew* how Darcy's neighbors and friends would react to her being taken away in cuffs. Just like she knew that, although Kyle's was the only name on the lease, the loft had been her home too. Her safe sanctuary away from the memories.

Margo had stolen that from her.

Even worse, Margo had forced her family—the family Darcy had come to consider her own—to abandon Darcy at her lowest point. Her stomach hollowed out whenever she thought back to those first few months. How she'd cried until she had no tears left to give and how, at night, the terrifying loneliness would creep in and take hold.

Every cruel word spoken and every betrayal against Darcy came rushing back.

Nope, the only question Darcy should be asking herself was why she hadn't moved further away.

Chapter Four

For a guy who was supposed to be the self-appointed spokesman for the Eastons, keeping an eye on the prize instead of Darcy's ass would have been a smart move. Instead, he was so busy appreciating the heart-shaped perfection pointed in his direction from behind the rose garden, he nearly made a tactical error.

Darcy wasn't the goal, securing his family's happiness was. Something his brain had always known, but his heart had a hard time accepting. Gage wasn't an expert by any means, but he was pretty sure that spark he'd felt the other day was more than just a lingering attraction. Or nostalgia from a happier time.

Reason enough to forgo hand delivering the new offer, and head straight for the mail slot. The envelope contained personal assurances from Rhett about the venue and caliber of personnel he'd be bringing in.

It also included an apology from Gage. Not for Kyle, or his family, or anything that he wasn't a part of. That wasn't his place. He just apologized for his behavior yesterday.

It had been a long time since he'd seen her, and while he'd managed to put most of his emotions behind him, after writing that letter—all eleven drafts—the curiosity of what could have been was still strong enough to give him pause.

There was no point in picking up where they left off, especially because when they left off she was about to marry his brother. But there was nothing wrong with taking a moment to enjoy the view. And what a view it was.

Denim clad cheeks, the perfect palm full, attached to a pair of mile-long legs that, at one time, had been a regular co-star in his fantasies. Shit, what was he thinking?

They'd played a pretty significant role in last night's dream—only they weren't encased in anything but his sheets—making for one hell of a tense and uncomfortable morning. Reason number one for canceling his lunch meeting and driving out to Belle Mont House. No matter how dangerous seeing her again could be, now that he'd seen her, he couldn't walk away.

Reason two was sealed in an envelope, burning a hole in his jacket pocket.

Then there was reason three. That look on her face when he'd walked away yesterday. Confused, scared, resigned.

He'd seen her wear that sad as fuck smile before, but he'd never been the cause of it. Until now. And that didn't sit right. Watching her put on a brave smile in the face of devastation had always called out to every protective instinct he owned, but being the devastating force felt like a sword to the gut.

Gage couldn't be the guy to light up that smile, but he refused to be another person in her life to cast more shadows.

Letter in hand, he walked up the wide steps of the old Victorian and took the letter out of his pocket. He stuck it in the slot, but immediately pulled it back out and straightened.

"It's a piece of paper that could change her life," he said, calling himself all kinds of pussy. "A win-win, asshole, so just drop the offer in the slot and be done with it."

Only, when he stuck it in the front door, his fingers refused to let go. Why? Because, like the bonehead he was, Gage didn't want to be done with it. From the beginning, his relationship with Darcy had been a series of unfinished business. And if he slid that letter through the slot, it would be reopening that door—and everything that came with it.

He'd long ago given up on the idea of them, and he didn't need to tempt fate by opening the door that had been hell to seal.

"Are you looking to get married?"

The letter slipped out of his fingers and Gage spun around. "Holy shi—"

He caught himself before he let a blue streak of adult words run loose, because standing in front of him was no adult. Nope, light brown pigtails, pink tutu, freckles—and a frosting mustache that spoke of a recent sugar fix.

He hadn't spent enough time around kids to even guess at her age, but this stealth ballerina was travel-sized enough to have him censoring his words.

"'Cuz, if you're looking to get married, we're closed." With a cute shrug, she pointed over his shoulder to the antique Closed sign on the door behind him.

Gage peered down through the glass panes of the ornate door to the envelope sitting on the marble entry, casually laying between the water bill and an ad for a free carpet cleaning, and his stomach rolled. He tried the door. Locked.

He tried it harder—still locked.

Shit.

"Do you get paid to sneak up on customers?" he asked, wondering if he could slip his arm in the slot and get the envelope back. Because now that he didn't have a choice, he knew he'd made the wrong one.

"My mommy says I'm light on my feet," she said, swaying from side to side. "It's what makes me a good dancer."

To prove her point, she put her hands over her head and did some kind of complicated turn with a few feet-stomping actions in there. Gage thought maybe it was ballet with some tap thrown in. But what the hell did he know about dance?

"Nice." Eyes back on the envelope, he knelt down and pushed the mail flap open. His hands were so big he couldn't even squeeze them past the knuckles. It was like the Hulk trying to get the last Pringle.

Tiny stood behind him, watching over his shoulder, her hot cake breath on the back of his neck making his palms sweat.

"You know what else makes a good dancer?" There was no point in answering, the girl was already talking again. "Glitter."

A tiny hand flew in front of his face, then did some sort of shimmering movement, which, the girl was right—the early summer sun glistened off her pink sparkly fingernails. Her teeny, tiny, could-fit-inside-the-mail-slot fingers.

Gage straightened, then smiled. Tiny smiled back.

"You're a ballerina, aren't you? Yeah, I could tell. I saw this documentary on ballerinas a few years back. They were dressed like you, minus the sparkles though. Real athletes, those women. And they talked about being light on their feet—"

"What's a documentary?"

A throbbing started behind his right eye. "You know, like a movie or a TV show, but it teaches you things."

"Like Angelina Ballerina?"

"Yeah, like that," he said and, *great*, now he was lying to small children. "Anyway, they said that although feet were important, it was also about the arms. Ballerina's needed to have small arms." He thought about what kind of complex *that* might give a growing girl, then added, "Small but strong arms, that can fit in small, tight places."

She crinkled her nose. "Like through a hoop?"

"Sure." He looked at the mail slot. "Or tight spaces like that. Can you reach through there?"

"Ah huh," she said, but instead of fetching him the letter, she took off giggling down the stairs.

"Hey, Tiny," Gage called after her. "Where are you going?"

"To get my mom and tell her you're trying to steal her mail."

Shit!

At least she wasn't fetching her dad to tell him some crazy creeper was asking about her small arms. "It's not her mail, well the top one isn't. It's mine. I accidently dropped it in the slot without, ah, signing it."

Tiny stopped at the bottom step, turned back around, and gave him a look that implied she thought he was full of shit. And he was. But he was also desperate. "Can you help me? No point in giving a letter if it isn't signed."

He watched her consider her options: help the stranger or run for help. And just when he thought she was going to walk on the wild side, her eyes drifted to the right—not to the house where her mom, the cook or maybe the cute assistant he'd met the other day was—but to the rose garden, where Darcy was holding a bouquet of roses, pink like Tiny's tutu, her face frozen in horror.

Everything in his brain seemed to freeze, unable to put together the logical pieces, as he stood paralyzed on the porch of Darcy's house.

Her home, she'd called it.

Darcy called out, most likely to her little girl, because Tiny turned her head back toward Gage, and when he met those piercing blue eyes head on, his heart stopped—right there in his chest. It gave one hard thump of recognition, then nothing.

Time slowed, rewound to a place where every pain felt fresh, raw, so insurmountable he had to question if what he saw, and what he felt, lined up. It was as if his entire body was holding its breath, waiting for his mind and his heart to search all of the implications, all of the possibilities, and come up with an answer that made sense.

The cute nose, caramel ringlets, and dusting of freckles were all Darcy's. But those eyes—and this was where the anger made way for anguish—*Jesus,* those eyes were Easton blue. Filled with excitement and mischief and a little bit of attitude. Even that crooked smile, which said she knew she was in trouble for talking to a stranger but it was worth it, was all Kyle.

A feeling too difficult to articulate and so unfamiliar overwhelmed him as he struggled to get his emotions under control.

"Hey, Tiny. You never told me your name," he managed past the lump in his throat.

Tiny looked over her shoulder once more, then gave him a toothy grin that damn near made him weep. "Kylie. What's yours?"

Kylie.

Gage took a step forward, then eased down on the top step, afraid his knees would buckle.

Kyle had a kid.

And Gage had a niece. Who was bright, and beautiful, and liked frosting and all things dancing. Yet, he didn't know anything else about her.

Not a damn thing.

"Gage," he pushed out through the emotion squeezing his throat. "My name's Gage."

"Gage is that old friend I was telling you about," Darcy said, her heels clicking up the brick pathway as she took a defensive stance behind her daughter.

Gage wanted to say he was her uncle, and he was sorry for not being there for her, that he didn't know. He didn't fucking know. But he didn't want to scare her, or stir up more animosity with Darcy, so he just smiled like his heart wasn't in his throat.

"The one you were sad about?" Kylie asked Darcy, her little voice all sweet concern.

Gage looked at Darcy, watched a broad wave of emotions tear through her dark brown pools and his gut knotted. From fear to relief, even some of that sadness Tiny was hinting at, it was all there, right beneath that heart-wrenching plea she was sending his way.

Please don't hurt her. You can hurt me, but not her.

And wasn't that a sad state of affairs. That her first thought, with regards to him, was that he'd hurt her. Hurt them.

He hadn't meant to back then. And sure as hell hadn't meant to now. But it was clear that she wasn't happy he was back. Well, he wasn't exactly happy about his reasons for coming either, or his five-year delay, but he was there now. And he intended to make it count.

"I never meant to make you sad, Darcy."

Darcy's heart lumbered painfully at the words she'd waited so long to hear. She'd waited five years for a moment like this, to hash out the past and finally move on. But out of the countless scenarios she'd mentally played out, never once in all that time had she imagined that her reunion with Gage would take place in front of the one person it could hurt the most.

"Honey," she said, giving her daughter's shoulders a gentle squeeze. "Why don't you go grab your dance bag so we're not late for class."

Kylie turned those big blue eyes Darcy's way. "But I want to meet your friend."

Gage swallowed so hard at the innocent comment that Darcy heard it. Felt his emotion swell and expand, until all she could process was the anxious thump of his heart. She was startled to realize it wasn't anger or blame Gage was radiating.

But anguish and heartache.

"Maybe next time," she said, and then sent Kylie off with a gentle pat to the bum.

"Bye, Mister."

"Until next time, Tiny," he said, standing, as Kylie skipped up the step, her tutu bouncing. She grabbed the handle and gave it a twist, then bumped it with her hip.

"Hey, I thought you said it was locked."

"Nope, I said we were closed. You got to jiggle it just right." Kylie gave one of her playful grins that, God bless her, had Gage smiling back.

Kylie ran into the house, slamming the front door behind her, the sound echoing in its finality. Gage and Darcy stood silent, each second more painful than the last, and despite the warm temperature, a cold chill swept through her body.

When she was certain they were completely alone, she said, "If you came to talk about the wedding—"

"Fuck the wedding." He turned those intense blue eyes her direction and she felt the full force of his anger. "I couldn't give a rat's ass about policies and family feuds right now."

"I never meant for it to happen like this."

Gage didn't move, just stood there in that still way he had, keeping his emotions in check. Even when he was angry, he considered the effect his actions could have. That's where he differed from his twin. "That implies you had some kind of plan that didn't include hiding her from us forever."

"I didn't hide her," Darcy defended, and it was the truth. "You all shut *me* out. I called you, I texted."

"You called me once," he said harshly. "Once, Darcy. A few hours after you left Kyle standing at the altar, and I was too busy dealing with three hundred confused guests to answer. And maybe if you'd started the text with, 'Hey, I'm sorry. By the way, I'm pregnant and it's Kyle's,' I might have called you back, but again, by that point I was too deep in funeral shit and my family's grief to see straight."

"A funeral your mom had me escorted out of," she said, because *wow*, that still had the power to hurt. She'd long ago accepted that she wasn't part of the Eastons anymore, but hearing it solidified things. "Escorted out like I didn't have the right to grieve the man who I'd loved enough to want to marry."

"But you didn't marry him."

"No, I didn't, and I'm not sorry about that," she said, and Gage stepped back as if she'd slapped him. "I'm not sorry that I walked away from a marriage that was doomed, and I'm not sorry that I chose to put Kylie's happiness first. Someone had to. But I am sorry that I didn't try harder to tell you about Kylie."

At her admission, his eyes flickered to the ground, but not before she saw a flash of relief. Shoving his hands in his pockets, like he used to when he'd get nervous, he asked, "Why didn't you? Tell me about her. I mean, after she was born."

"I didn't know how," she admitted. "At first I was so busy dealing with Kyle's death and trying to figure out how to be a single mom, and before I knew it a year had passed."

"But it's been four years, Pink," he said, the sound of her nickname on his lips making her heart do a slow roll in her chest. "Four years of memories and moments, four years of Kylie not knowing that she had more family out there who wanted to love her."

"Kylie knows she has uncles," Darcy said. "We talk about her dad, his brothers, how we met in college, and how he always managed to turn a bad situation into a party. Her favorite story is the New Year we all got snowed in and we had cake for breakfast lunch and dinner, because it was the only thing Kyle bought at the store."

Gage relaxed slightly, though his expression was the same anguish fueled one he'd worn at the funeral. And Darcy felt a most annoying tug to walk into his arms and talk about how much she missed those days. How much she'd missed him.

That he looked like he could use a hug too didn't help—not that she planned on giving him one. She was afraid that once she was in his arms she'd let her guard down, hand over some of the stress. And then when he walked, and he would, she'd be right back where she'd been five years ago.

Without a word, he let out a tired breath and turned to look out at the rose garden, taking in their small cottage and the tire swing hanging from the old oak tree. Belle Mont House, with its acres of land, stunning city views, and homey feel was the perfect setting to raise a child, to instill security and confidence, and imagination.

She wondered what Gage saw when he looked out. What he'd think, when he got past the anger, of the life she'd built for herself and for Kylie.

"I get that you were hurt," he finally said. "But how could you keep her from us? From Kyle?"

"How could I not?" she defended. "Your mother had me arrested, accused me of using Kyle for his money, then sued me for the engagement ring." She could tell by the look on Gage's face that he didn't know about the last part. "Yeah, she had me served at my workplace, in the middle of a corporate event. My boss was not pleased, and I was humiliated." She shivered at the memory. "I couldn't bring Kylie into all of that."

She paused, knowing what she was about to say would hurt, but knowing that the only way to start the healing on both sides was the truth. "Kyle knew I was pregnant. I told him the day I found out. It was why we sped up the wedding date."

She watched as Gage slowly met her gaze, his own full of disbelief and unprecedented disappointment. He stared at her for a long moment, studying her as if he had something important to say, something that could make it all make sense, but when he opened his mouth, nothing came out.

"He wasn't ready," she said quietly

"He told you that?" He sounded so lost Darcy placed a hand on his arm, and this time he didn't jerk away.

"He showed me," she said, remembering how he'd promised to stop the cheating, be the kind of husband and dad they deserved. Only he hadn't broken up with the intern, hadn't stopped the late nights after, hadn't lived up to his promise. So Darcy had walked, told him that he blew it as a husband, but he still had a chance to be a great dad, and that maybe they'd be better as co-parents than a couple.

But he'd blown that too.

"He actually said he wasn't ready to be a dad?" Gage asked, disbelief thick.

"What kind of dad-to-be gets plastered enough to wrap his car around a tree, without a second thought of how it would affect his child?" Darcy said. "I didn't want that legacy for Kylie. She didn't deserve to grow up with the aftermath of all of our choices. Her happiness was my number one focus. It always will be." She looked him dead in the eye. "Which is why I need you to leave."

"No way." He stepped back. "You can't drop all of that on me and then expect to just disappear."

"I'm not disappearing, Gage. I'm taking my daughter to dance class, and trying to avoid her walking into this." She gestured to the aggressive stance he'd adopted. "Because that's what mothers do."

Chapter Five

"What part of no legal standing, did you misunderstand?"

Gage grabbed a beer from the fridge and shoved Rhett over so he could sit—on his own couch.

He took a long swallow, but it didn't help. The sharp ache in his chest that had started the moment he'd realized Kylie was his niece, had only increased as the day had gone on. Coming home to find his brothers sprawled out on his couch, drinking his beer, and demanding answers he didn't have, only made things worse.

He didn't even want to acknowledge the dog cozied up on his leather recliner, wearing a Seahawks jersey and chewing on a bone twice the size of his head.

"Then let's talk to another lawyer," Josh, the oldest brother, and mediator of the family, said. He was dressed in his usual suit and tie, slicked up and looking like he'd just come home from dinner with the mayor—which being Portland's most influential DA, he probably had. "A better one who will give us some actual answers."

"I called three of the best family law attorneys in Portland," Gage said, resting his head against the back of the couch. "Unless the parents are found unfit, they maintain full custody over the child. And since the father is deceased, full custody falls to the mother, who is Darcy."

"So she can stop us from ever seeing our niece, stop Mom from knowing her only grandchild?" Owen, the hot head of the group asked, pouring himself two fingers of scotch. "That's bullshit."

"That's the law." Gage grabbed the bottle. "And that had better not be my good stuff."

Owen took a sip, then leaned back, setting his socked feet on the coffee table. "You mean the one you keep hidden in the laundry room?"

"Dad gave me that." Gage grabbed the bottle, then shoved his brother's feet to the floor.

Owen might be the biggest of the brothers, and with his buzzed head and body art, he looked more like a bouncer than an up-scale bar owner, but he was starting to piss Gage off.

"What defines unfit? Because to me she became unfit the second she decided to keep Kyle's kid from us," Rhett said.

"She didn't keep her from us. He's even listed on the birth certificate as the father," Gage said, now knowing the truth. He hadn't just called a lawyer. He'd hired a PI to look into Kylie's birth. And what he'd uncovered didn't just leave Gage with more questions, it made him wonder what Kyle had been thinking that night.

"The hell she didn't. Naming Kyle as the dad isn't the same as telling us. And what about the hospital? Aren't they obligated to contact the baby's family?"

"They did contact Kylie's family. According to the law, Darcy is the girl's only family," he said, although it sure as hell didn't feel like that. Gage had spent less than ten minutes with her, and already she'd taken up space in his heart. Being around her was like having more time with his brother.

It would be like that for all of them. So Gage understood their frustration, but he also understood that it was a group effort that had gotten them to this point.

"Well, then maybe we should pay Darcy a visit, and remind her that Kylie has more family," Owen said.

"Right, because a united front worked so well for us in the past," Clay said, and Gage was thankful that one of them was thinking sanely.

"Well, we have to do something," Rhett argued, standing to pace the room. "Kyle would have wanted us in her life. She needs someone who will tell her how amazing her dad was, how he was driven and funny, and a standup guy. She needs to hear all of that."

"Darcy is treating Kyle's memory with respect," Gage said, wondering why telling what he believed to be the truth felt like a betrayal to his brother.

"I'm sorry," Rhett said. "Did you learn that in the two minutes she actually talked to you or was it when that ass of hers walked away from you, again, and you started wondering why you never got to tap that?"

"Fuck you, Rhett!" Gage's head was spinning over his brother betraying his confidence like that. He'd confessed his feelings for Darcy in a low moment, when he thought the circle of brotherly trust was in play between the two of them. "I only went back there because you asked me to."

And that was the truth.

Arguing with his brothers didn't feel right. Arguing about Kyle with them? That felt toxic. But looking for someone to blame wouldn't help anyone. Been there, done that, and they'd all lost out.

Gage wasn't about to let that happen again.

"Kyle knew that Darcy was pregnant," he said, having a hard time swallowing the truth. "And before you go saying that she could have lied, I already checked. Kyle paid an extra fee to have Darcy added to his medical insurance. Why would he do that if she would be automatically added when they got married?"

"She was working as a contractor back then, maybe she didn't have insurance," Josh speculated.

That's what Gage had thought too. "A month before the wedding, Kyle started a college fund with ten thousand dollars in it."

Rhett took a step back and sat heavily on the couch, the wind and fight knocked right out of him.

"I would have found it when I was combing through his estate," Josh said, but he didn't sound as confident as he had a moment ago. Gage felt for his big brother.

Gage and Kyle might have been polar opposites when it came to personality and interests, but as twins they shared everything. Or at least Gage thought they had. But after the past few days, he was beginning to wonder what else Kyle had kept from the family.

What else he'd kept from Gage.

"Kyle set it up with the beneficiary being Darcy, and, no, she hasn't touched a cent." Which was even more impressive, since he now knew how much debt she'd taken on with Belle Mont.

"That still doesn't change the fact that we missed out on several crucial years," Clay said, and out of all of the brothers, Gage knew that this was hitting him the hardest.

Clay looked up to Kyle, even followed him off to college. And it was clear by the haunted expression on his face, Clay was beginning to question things about his big brother that might change everything.

"No, it doesn't," Gage said, pulling out four more tumblers. "And I don't know if she did what she thought was best for Kylie, or if she was acting out of anger. We all could have handled things differently back then." Gage poured two fingers in each glass. "But at this point, the only thing that matters is getting the chance to know Kylie, and going at her balls out and fists swinging at her mother won't win us uncles of the year."

"Then we change our approach," Josh said, taking his glass. "She wants to plan the wedding; let her plan Rhett's wedding. Between the cake tasting and picking out flowers, it will give him time to see what's going on, and find the best way to convince her we just want to know our niece."

"Are you kidding?" Gage said. "What about Mom?"

"I think Mom would rather meet her granddaughter than have Darcy gone from the property," Rhett said, getting on board.

"I agree," Clay said, leaning forward to pick up his scotch. "Which is why I'm willing to throw in a signing bonus if she agrees to plan this wedding." Before Gage could argue that it wouldn't work, Clay held up a hand. "I don't have anything against Darcy. I just want to see my niece, and I want Mom to know Kyle's kid, I think that's what Kyle would have wanted."

Uncertainty coursed through Gage's body at such a swift pace he could taste it. If that was what Kyle wanted, then he should have told them. This was exactly like five years ago, everyone acting in Kyle's best interests, when Gage still wasn't sure why he hadn't told them. "I already told you, money has never been a motivator."

Clay picked up a piece of paper and scribbled an amount on it, then slid it across the coffee table. "I think this will go a long way toward finding out some answers."

Rhett picked it up and looked at the sum and nodded. "I'll double that. The only problem is I leave tomorrow for New York. I'm in the recording studio all week and Stephanie is headed to LA. I was going to have Mom deal with the planner, but that's no longer an option."

All four brothers looked at Gage and a bad feeling started to coil in his gut. "No, I am not planning your wedding."

"I'm not asking you to plan my wedding. Between Steph's Pinterest board and her Wedding Binder, it's all planned out. What I am asking," Rhett leaned back, his grin too wide to be anything but trouble, "is for you to get to know Darcy again, remind her that we aren't assholes, and find out what it will take to get on her good side."

"You always said the key to closing a deal was to know the client's weakness." Clay held his tumbler in the air in a toast. "If you don't think it's financial, then here's to finding out what it is."

"Oh," Rhett said. "You get to tell Mom."

⁂

"A hundred thousand dollars?" Jillian said, piping numbers on every one of the two dozen jersey-inspired cupcakes.

It was the first Tiny Tykes football meet of the new season, and with Sam being the Bull Frog's newest member, Darcy had offered to help with the after party. She'd thrown lots of kids parties in the past; it was how she paid her way through college—well, that and dressing up like a clown. But managing twenty five-year olds in cleats and shoulder pads, double the amount of helicopter parents, and a cheerleader who refused to trade in the tutu for pompoms, was enough to give even the most experienced of planners a rash.

Darcy picked up a waffle cone, filled it with fruit salad, and stuck it in the serving tray, fashioned from an old egg carton. "That was their counter offer, and it just covers my fee."

"That would go a long way toward paying down the loan," Jillian said, and Darcy thought about the septic tank, the AC, and just what she could do with that much money. "Who are they bringing in for entertainment?"

Darcy rattled off a few of the names from Gage's email, and Jillian slapped a hand over her mouth. "Are you kidding?" she said through her frosted fingers. "That sounds like the lineup for this year's Grammies."

Darcy understood her friend's excitement. Having a VIP list of that caliber, having them come and spend an evening at Belle Mont would send its popularity soaring. Overnight, her historic labor of love would become the premiere venue for events in the Pacific Northwest.

"I know. Makes it hard to say no, huh?"

"This is your dream, your business, your daughter. There is no wrong answer here." Jillian placed the cupcakes on a green felt board, lining them up in a starting position. "Out of curiosity, what did you say?"

Darcy closed her eyes and willed her stomach to stop churning. "That I'd be willing to talk about it."

"Oh my God." Jillian said, taking Darcy's hand and jumping up and down. "Oh my God! This is so exciting. Rhett Easton and that stellar butt of his, which I believe was voted best backside of the year in *People Magazine*, is going to marry Stephanie Stone at Belle Mont House. This is huge!"

"I still haven't said yes."

"But saying you're thinking about it is like a yes in Darcy-land. You're too sweet to give people false hope." Jillian stopped. "So why aren't you jumping?"

"I found the letter," she admitted, feeling like a loser.

Any smart businesswoman would know when a contract that had the potential to put your company on the map said, *Please discard the earlier letter,* they wouldn't go in search of the letter. They'd put their emotions aside, sign on the dotted line, and take their daughter to Disneyland to celebrate.

But once Darcy knew there was a letter, she couldn't sleep until she'd found it. And when she found it, buried among her bills, and saw that it was written in Gage's writing, she cracked the seal. It didn't take a genius to guess what she'd done next.

So, yes, she was too emotional right then to be smart.

Jillian took the cone out of her hand, that was cracked and dripping blueberries onto the grass, and tossed it in the trash bin. "You want to talk about it?"

"No."

"You sure?" Jillian placed a cupcake on a napkin and sat on the park bench behind them. "You look like you want to talk about it."

"Maybe."

Jillian waved the cupcake in the air, then patted the bench next to her.

"Fine, I want to talk about it." Darcy took a seat next to her friend, took the cupcake, and took a big bite. "He ruined what should have been an easy yes." She looked out at the herd of laughing kids, her eyes immediately zeroing in on Kylie. In her tutu and cheer shirt, she was chasing a group of boys around the bounce house. "He said he was sorry."

"That jerk," she teased.

"He made it personal. Took what was supposed to be a simple business decision and added all of these warm fuzzies to it."

"Warm fuzzies? That must have been some note."

"Rhett might be the songwriter, but Gage was always good with words." Darcy opened the note she'd tucked in her dress pocket. Unfolding it, her hands shook as the faint scent of cologne and Gage escaped into the warm summer breeze. She ran her finger across its edge, then released a deep breath.

"He wrote you notes a lot then?" Jillian questioned, sounding a little too suspicious.

"In a notebook," she defended. "Nothing big. I had this composition book in college."

"Like that?" Jillian pointed to a black notebook on the picnic table. It had a worn spine, tabs sticking out the top, and fabric swatches hanging from the bottom. It was how she put together an event, collected her ideas and designs.

"Exactly like that, except this one was for taking notes in my calculus class. I hated calculus, and Gage was great with numbers."

"Great with words, great with numbers, and you chose the self-centered philanderer?"

Darcy ignored this. "Every time he'd come to my dorm room, he'd write some silly note in the margins for me to find the next day. It was this thing we had."

"And you never dated?"

"No," Darcy said, smiling at the question they'd received a million times over the years. "He wasn't looking to get married, and a guy would be insane not to marry me." She looked up. "That's what he used to tell people."

Jillian gave a disbelieving snort. "Did he have to tug your ponytail to make you wonder if there was more there?"

"Oh, I had a thing for him when we first met, but he had a long-time girlfriend, then Kyle came for a visit and he charmed me into a date." She shrugged. "Gage was all for it. Said I needed to get out and have some fun. Then Kyle and I started dating and people stopped asking, and well—"

"Here you are all these years later, and he wrote you a note?"

Darcy looked at the words once again and that strange humming, the one that had started when she unintentionally felt him up during their fall, came back. "It's a good note."

Darcy handed it over to her friend. She didn't need to read it again. She'd already memorized every curve and line.

D ~

I know I am a better man than my past actions have shown. It shames me to know that the one person who helped me through my father's death didn't benefit from the honorable man he raised me to be. A friend doesn't walk away without a goodbye, and you, Darcy, were one of the best I've ever had. You deserved more from me. And for that I am truly sorry.

~ G

Jillian finished, held up a finger so she could read it again, then slid another cupcake in front of Darcy. "That was a good note."

Without a word, Darcy pulled out the newest offer that Rhett had emailed last night and handed it to Jillian. "Now, read this again and tell me if you see a problem with it."

"I think *I* need a cupcake before I do." Grabbing Darcy's cupcake, her friend dove in, not coming up until the wrapper was licked clean, and she'd finished the contract.

"Oh, boy," Jillian said dramatically. "He said he was sorry, then gave you the wedding of a career, and a hundred-thousand-dollar venue fee." Jillian set the wrapper on the bench. "I mean, yes, it was clear there's no wiggle room on most all of his conditions, but I don't see a problem at all. You get demanding clients all the time. You are the Bridezilla's kryptonite."

"The email was titled, *We need to talk*. He never mentioned Kylie, but I know that's what he meant."

Jillian set down the contract. "You do need to talk. About a lot of things. He needs the chance to understand why you never told him about Kylie, and you need a chance to finally clear the air and get past the big Easton rain cloud that has been following you for five years."

It wasn't all the Eastons who had haunted her memories. More like one specific Easton.

Gage.

"But that isn't the Gage I knew," she said, pointing to the contract. "That guy is calculating, unwavering, and cold." She held up the note and felt her resolve soften. "This is the Gage I remember. The one who was humble and honest, and always did the right thing, no matter how hard. The guy who would never use his family's name and money for leverage. This is the guy who I miss."

The guy who would know that, although Darcy might make her own mistakes, she didn't need a hundred-thousand-dollar bribe to set things right.

"He told me to disregard the apology, and offered me money." Exactly what Kyle would have done. What he had done—several times.

"What if the money had nothing to do with his apology?" Jillian offered, as if handling a dispute on the playground. "What if he apologized, then changed his mind in giving it to you because he didn't want it to get lumped in with your decision about Rhett's wedding?"

"Maybe." That did sound more like Gage, and took some of the sting out of his offer.

She hated to think that after all of the years of friendship, it would end with a signature on a contract and a payoff. Not that she'd been excited about the thought of having him back in her life, but after seeing him, and how much he looked like Kylie...

She shook her head. The similarities were astounding and had left her spinning with all of the possible what-ifs. She'd tried to keep busy, tried not to dwell on things that couldn't be changed. But in the middle of the night, when the house was quiet and Kylie was fast asleep, doubt would creep in. Take over until decisions she'd been confident in started to show their cracks.

Margo had accused her of marrying Kyle for his contacts and money. Only to dump him when his career took a nosedive. And she didn't want to prove the woman right.

Both his career and their engagement had taken a nosedive because he'd slept with his boss's daughter. And a six-figure bonus didn't erase the heartache the Eastons had put her through. It also didn't erase the fact that Kylie had a whole other family out there who she didn't know anything about.

"He wrote that note before he met Kylie, and his "disregard the apology" was his way of saying he thinks I made a mistake. What if he's right, what if I did make a mistake?"

The one bite of cupcake she gotten before Jillian stole it soured in her stomach.

Gage might have made a rash decision to end their friendship in a grief-clouded moment, but he was the most steadfast person Darcy knew. He wouldn't recant an apology, knowing it would hurt her, if he didn't believe she was truly at fault. And he wouldn't offer an outrageous amount of money unless he thought she'd be swayed by it.

"What if I let my pain and anger overshadow what was right for Kylie?"

"Stop!" Jillian yelled, jumping to her feet.

Startled, Darcy looked up just as Jillian cupped her hands to her mouth like a megaphone. "No cleats in the bounce house!"

"Okay, Auntie Jillian," Kylie hollered back, then proceeded to explain to each and every boy that they needed to remove their cleats.

"Seriously, you were worried about being a bad mom? Your four-year-old just took on boys twice her size and forced them into following the rules. And all with a smile. Trust me, you're doing a great job."

Darcy tossed the wrapper in the trash bin, then picked up a cone to finish with the fruit salad. "I know, it's just...I look at her and I see so much of Kyle in her. I want to make sure that I'm taking into consideration what he would have wanted too."

"But he isn't here. You are." Jillian took Darcy's hand. "And being a single parent means making all of the choices by yourself, and every once in a while you might make a wrong one. But I know you've never made decisions based on how it would hurt someone else. You've always done what's best for Kylie."

"I'd like to think that I have, but sometimes the right choice isn't so easy to see."

"No, it's not." Jillian opened a bag of sliced oranges and poured them into a bright green bowl. "But I promise you that at the time you made the decisions you did think they were the right ones. But life goes on, goals change, we grow, and sometimes what was best in that moment isn't the best thing now."

Jillian was right. Kyle's brothers might have turned their backs on Darcy, but they never would have walked away from Kylie. Which was a huge part of her reservations.

"Kyle's brothers are a force. His mother is a nightmare. And Gage looked so angry when we ended things the other day." She didn't even want to think about Margo's reaction. The woman would navigate from anger to resentment like a Formula-1 driver. No one did guilt and vengeance quite like Margo Easton. "Once they meet Kylie, there is no getting rid of the Eastons. Even if they make my life hell."

"It sounds like Gage reacted out of shock, and you can't blame the guy," Jillian reasoned. "That was a hard way to find out he had a niece."

"I know." Remembering his shocked expression was enough to forgive him of everything he'd said. "I should have handled it better back then, but I wasn't strong enough to face any more rejection."

"Strong enough? Honey, Hitler would have been scared of Margo Easton. She blamed her son's cheating on you, said you weren't woman enough, then sued you," Darcy's biggest cheerleader said. "I think you are a saint for even being open to her meeting Kylie."

"I don't want to keep her from Margo, I just don't want Margo's hate for me to affect Kylie."

"If you're afraid of Kylie getting stuck in the middle, or them making things hard on you, then meet them on neutral territory and voice your concerns," Jillian said. "That's what Jerry and I had to do when we separated, to make sure Sam didn't miss out because of our issues."

"You want me to sit down with all of them? Have you seen the Eastons together? They are like a gladiator team."

"Fine, then start with Gage. You said you were friends? Friendship is a great place to start. You can set the boundaries and the rules up front, leaving zero room for misunderstandings."

"And if Margo won't listen?"

Jillian's face took on a fierce expression that only came out when she was talking about her family—and she thought of Darcy and Kylie as hers. "In the end, you're Kylie's mom. Period. So what you say goes. Including who she gets to spend time with and how they spend that time. It's that simple."

Darcy snorted, because nothing with the Eastons was ever simple. They were the most intense group of men Darcy had ever met. But they were also big softies when it came to family. Darcy hated it when people held her responsible for Kyle's choices, so she refused to do the same.

"I'll email Gage when I get home, tell him we can meet to talk about Kylie. As for the wedding, I'll make it clear that it is a separate issue, and if we agree to move forward I'm not taking more than my asking rate."

"What about Kylie?" Jillian asked. "Are you going to bring her?"

Darcy's eyes once again found Kylie. She was in the bounce house, hands on her hips, chin in the air, telling the biggest kid on the football team that tackling in the bounce house wasn't nice play.

Darcy smiled. "That depends on which Gage shows up. I would love for the guy who wrote that note to meet Kylie. But if it is the cold and calculated one who sent that contract, then all bets are off. I don't screw around with my daughter's happiness."

She'd walked away from a marriage to ensure it. She'd take on the entire Easton clan if it meant protecting it.

Chapter Six

It was official. Gage needed a vacation.

He'd started his day at the gym, getting his ass handed to him by Clay as he attempted to keep pace with a freaking machine. Oh, Clay had given him a pep talk. One that included name calling and multiple demands to hand over his man-card. Then Owen had arrived, proving the theory behind mob mentality, and by the time Josh showed up with a booklet of bridal gown swatches, Gage flipped them the finger and hit the showers.

By eight, he couldn't feel his legs, but managed to stay upright while he got dressed and walked the three blocks to his office. Half-way there, he heard his phone ping and saw that it was an email from Darcy saying, I AM OPEN TO DISCUSSING THE POSSIBILITIES AT YOUR EARLIEST CONVENIENCE, and damn near sprinted to his car.

There was a list of possibilities they needed to discuss. Kylie for one. They needed to come to an agreement that included his family being in her life. A close second was the wedding. But the only possibilities his head wanted to entertain were ones that had to do with exploring the connection between them.

In fact, last night he'd come up with some pretty damn creative ones. All of which required no clothes, and none of which were real possibilities. Didn't stop him from running to his car like some anxious teenager though.

Calling himself a dozen kinds of asshole, he tossed his gym bag in the truck and slammed the door. A snarling sounded from inside his car, followed by a loud growl that sounded straight out of *Jurassic Park*. And not an herbivore either, it sounded like one of those raptor things was inside his car, making mincemeat of his seats.

Gage placed a hand over the window and peered in when—

"What the hell?"

Something lunged at his face, throwing itself against the door, teeth bared, little pink painted nails scratching against the glass.

"*Yip!Yip!Yip!Yip!*"

He glanced around the parking lot, but didn't see anyone. No laughing brothers, no Stephanie, no one he could give the abomination to. Nope, it was just him and Fancy—dressed in a pink top with a skirt that was a ruffle of silk flowers on his butt.

"You, off the leather!"

At his voice, Littleshit went from snarling to panting happily, his hot breath and wet nose marking up the window. Gage didn't even want to get into what his tongue was doing to the glass.

A post-it note was stuck in the weather stripping on the window. It was small, yellow, and so funny Gage wanted to punch a brother—didn't matter which one, since they were likely all in on the joke. He should have known something was up when half of his family showed up before daylight.

He tore the note off the window.

Be back a week from tomorrow. Dog food's in the front seat, outfits in the carrier, wee-wee pads on the floorboard. You're welcome.

~ Rhett

PS. I hear kids like dogs, so there's that…

"One wee-wee in my car and shit will get real. Understood?" Gage said, opening the door and scooping Fancy up, who licked his face. "As soon as I find out where your dad is, you're going back to him."

Fancy didn't give two shits. He caught sight of his reflection in the window and struggled to get free so he could annihilate it.

Gage suspended him in midair, his miniature legs going a million miles a minute.

With an empathetic chuckle for the guy's struggle, he pulled out his phone and dialed Rhett. Gage left a scathing voicemail, then dialed Clay. Ditto.

He went down the list as not a single one of them answered, but Fancy had tired himself out and was hanging from his hand, limp, his tongue dangling out the side of his mouth.

Gage considered calling his mom, but was about as excited about dog-sitting as he was about lying. And since he knew that call would require an apology for not calling often enough, a promise to have dinner this week, and a complete accounting of his day, he punted.

A stacked redhead walked by and gave Gage a once over, then smiled. "Cute dog."

"You want him?" Gage asked holding Littleshit out in offering. "He's... ah...laid back, potty trained, and belonged to a celebrity."

Red gave an amused smile, and Gage smiled back, dialing the charm to magnetic. Even Littleshit played along, lifting those big dark brown doggie eyes her way and giving a cute puppy sigh. "Aw, what's his name?"

Gage groaned. "Fancy."

Red bit her lip, trying not to laugh. "Fancy?"

"He's a real lap dog, would make a great house pet."

"Then why are you giving him away?"

"I'm allergic."

She laughed and unlocked her car door. "I thought it was because of the present *Fancy* left on the passenger side." With a wink, Red slammed her door and drove off.

Gage ducked down and that's when he saw the "present," sitting two inches from the wee-wee pad. With his most intimidating frown, he looked down at Fancy who was tucked against his side, fast asleep.

A few choice words later, the sleeping dog was in his carrier, the poo was in the wadded up wee-wee pad, and Gage was three rows over, depositing the present on the seat of Owen's motorcycle.

Climbing in his car, Gage called his secretary to cancel his morning appointments, then toyed with the idea of emailing Darcy back. But was afraid she'd pencil him in sometime after his niece graduated college. And he was tired of waiting...

For things to get easier, for the perfect time to reach out, for the universe to go pick on someone else for a while.

Gage's story was a series of right girl wrong time, and he was no closer to figuring out what to do about the attraction than when he'd first met her seven years ago. So he'd kept his distance, dating other women, playing the friend card. It had been the right move, and Gage liked to consider himself a good guy.

But it was no longer about him and her, or whatever unsettled business still lay between them. This was about family, so he snapped in his co-pilot and started the car.

Twenty minutes later, he was driving up the steep and winding streets of West Hills, passing by some of the oldest homes in the area. Turning down the brick road, which was lined on either side by the dozens of heritage crepe myrtle trees and led to Belle Mont House, Gage smiled fondly.

She was driven, he'd give her that. Darcy had done what so many other developers had failed. She'd resurrected one of Portland's oldest landmarks and brought back its glory. And she'd done it all on her own.

He parked in front of the main house and stepped out of the car, greeted by the gentle scent of rose petals and moss, which clung to the white oak trees scattered around the property. It had been a while since he'd spent a day away from the office and out in the sunshine. The sound of the rustling leaves was enough to bring a sense of calm that had been—

"*Yip!*"

Gage closed his eyes and counted to three—he'd intended to go all the way to ten, but after his nap, Fancy was rearing to go.

Gage scooped the dog out of his cage and clipped his leash on before setting him on the brick path. Fancy went to work sniffing the tires, the nearby tree, then the wide front porch step. Where he lifted a leg and did some more business. This one didn't require a cleanup, but irritated Gage all the same.

"Nice first impression," Gage said, ignoring that his hadn't come off any better. "Between the high pitched bark and that frilly shit you wear, all of the girl dogs are going to start asking if you had your boys clipped."

Fancy whipped his head, so his ears went to the side like he was in a boy band. Then he sat, poised, cleaning his dainty little paw.

"With all of the chick magnet dogs out there, I get you."

"Yip!"

"If you're good, I'll take you to the mall and buy you some flannel, or maybe one of those 'Bitches Love Me' T-shirts."

With a gentle tug, Dog Wonder-ful pranced up the steps and into the house, a bell jingling behind them. The front room was impressive, mahogany floors and wainscoting, with ornate molding around the ceilings and dramatic arches. The furniture was turn of the century, the chandelier tiffany, and the windows original leaded glass, which cast a rainbow glow around the room.

Belle Mont House wasn't just historic—it was a piece of art.

Gage looked at the hand painted details around each of the balusters, and tried to picture Darcy in jeans and an old college tee—her hair in a messy ponytail, her hands speckled in paint. He'd always liked Messy Darcy, almost as much as he liked Warm and Soft Darcy. But his new favorite, he decided, as he pushed through the back door of the house, was Polished Darcy in her business-ready blouses, slim fitted skirts that hugged her curves and ended just below the knee, exposing those mile-long legs of hers. Which were always finished off in a pair of fantasy inspiring pumps.

Today the blouse was buttoned, the skirt cream, and those pumps fuck-me red. And the relaxed smile on her pretty face said she hadn't seen him yet.

She stood at the head of the table, looking poised and confident, with a presentation easel behind her that read, HEIRLOOM BLOOMERS. CELEBRATING 100 YEARS OF FLORA HERITAGE.

"We could set up tables throughout the rose garden. Six-seater round tables in a cluster so that the group is kept together, but yet still invites intimate conversations," she said to the table of ladies in the gazebo.

Not ladies, Gage corrected. Seniors. In flowered dresses, pearled gloves, and hats worthy of a British royal wedding. A table full of them, sipping tea from elegant cups and eating sandwiches fit for a dog.

"That sounds ideal," a woman with bright pink lipstick and two matching circles painted on her cheeks said. "And where would you propose placing the flower stands?"

"We could always go traditional and have them set up around the lawn. Or we could get innovative and," Darcy removed the front poster board to expose a blown-up blueprint of Belle Mont's first floor, with red dots scattered strategically throughout, "move the show inside."

Several gasps escaped, followed by a chorus of whispers—some excited, some skeptical.

"I know that you have had the rose show outside for several decades, but your organization was founded by Ms. Pitman and her three best friends as a way to share ideas and celebrate their blooms. Their first ever Heirloom Bloomers Tea was held in Ms. Pitman's sunroom," Darcy said, silencing the group. "By moving it back indoors, it will allow *us* to spotlight each and every entry, and *rose enthusiasts* to take a leisurely walk back in time, admiring rose blooms whose roots date back several generations, in the way Ms. Pitman had originally imagined. A coming together of friends and neighbors."

"I do love the sound of that," a lady in bifocals, holding a cane said. "But our tables are much too big, they'd block the hallway."

"Excellent observation, Connie," Darcy said. "Which is why I have spoken with a local contractor, who's willing to build some vintage looking flower pedestals at a discounted price."

Gage looked down at Fancy, who was straining on the leash, trying to get loose so he could go greet everyone with a proper doggie hello. "We're going back inside to wait until her meeting is over. No wee-wee pads in there, so if you have to go, you hold it. Understood?"

"*Yip!*"

All dozen sets of eyes turned his way at the bark, including Darcy's. They went big with surprise, before taking a slow discovery of his body, only to stop when they reached Littleshit and narrow into two pissed off slits.

"Real smooth entrance," he whispered to the dog, who barked and went back to yanking at the leash. "No licking and no crotch sniffing. We'll go in like gentlemen and charm her into giving us a second chance."

Making his way down the back steps, Fancy trotting like he was a thoroughbred and this was the winner's lap at the Kentucky Derby, Gage greeted the table, "Morning, ladies. We didn't mean to interrupt your party."

"Well, a party isn't a party until the gentlemen arrive," a portly woman in her seventies said, pulling out a lace fan and cooling her cheeks. "And aren't you quite the specimen. Are you the contractor?" She looked at Darcy. "Is he the contractor?"

Gage's biceps flexed a bit, along with his ego, and Darcy snorted. "He doesn't know a thing about construction. Probably doesn't even own a tool belt."

"It isn't about how many tools a man has in his belt, it's how well he uses the tools he has," Gage said, his lips curving up into a smile when Darcy's face turned an adorable shade of pink.

"If you ask me, it's about how well he looks in a tool belt." Connie gave one more slow look, then winked. "I say you're hired. Have a seat next to me."

Gage winked back and Darcy rolled her eyes, but not before taking a thorough once-over of her own. Lingering extra-long, he noticed, on his tool belt.

"Unfortunately, Gage isn't on Belle Mont's approved list of service providers," Darcy said, her smile sweet as icing, her gaze dialed to castrate. "And he needs to get going. I'm sure he has a busy day ahead of him."

"Actually, I cleared my morning for our appointment."

"What appointment?"

"The one where we talk about me getting on your approved service provider list," he said, loving how she refused to laugh. Her lips were straining, she was so determined not to give in. "I've been trying to sweet talk my way onto that list for quite some time now, with no luck." He sat at the table, making himself comfortable. "Maybe you ladies can give me some pointers, help me figure out exactly what Darcy's looking for."

Connie patted down her hat and hair. "Well, aren't you determined and diligent. And absolutely delicious."

Gage winked again—this time at Darcy. "I aim to please."

"Ladies, would you excuse us?" Darcy asked, walking towards the house and snagging Gage by the elbow on her way. "The dog stays."

Fancy huffed in defiance, but didn't dare follow as Darcy led Gage silently through the back door, across the ballroom, not stopping until they were standing in the kitchen.

"Nice place," he said, taking in the room. It was large and open, the deep sunken farm sink and vintage cooking utensils adding the right amount of charm to the sleek, professional work areas, which could rival some of the top restaurants in Portland.

"Cut the crap, Gage." She folded her arms, which did amazing things to her blouse. Pulling the material, and tightening the buttons until all it would take was a simple flick of the finger for one to pop. "We didn't have an appointment, so why are you here?"

He pulled his phone out, swiped to his email, and read, "I am open to discussing the possibilities at your earliest convenience." He pocketed it.

"I thought you'd email back, not just show up before I could—"

"Make other plans?"

"No," she said, but for the first time since he'd arrived, she broke eye contact. "To check my calendar. I'm in the middle of a meeting."

"You said at your earliest convenience, and I conveniently had this morning open." He pulled out a chair and sat down. "I don't mind waiting."

Gage had sat at Darcy's table a thousand times on a thousand different occasions. But there was something about him sitting at this table that had Darcy on edge.

She narrowed those sharp, brown eyes at him then pulled out her own chair, and sat. "I have a meeting directly following this one. Now will be fine," she said, not sounding the least bit fine with her current predicament.

Gage prided himself in his ability to control even the most stressful of situations while putting people at ease. His mother claimed his need to please was a direct result of middle child syndrome. Darcy had once told him that it stemmed from having a big heart. Which was why he'd started to take her uneasiness with his presence personally.

"I didn't come to make things worse. I came because we need to talk."

She let out a big sigh and sat back. "I know. And you were right, I would have kept postponing this, and if we intend to find a solution that works for everyone, we need to actually discuss it."

A small spark of hope swelled in his chest. He'd come in here expecting some kind of argument, but her body language, although tense, was very open. "Are you're considering our offer?"

"Parts of it," she said, and he just prayed that Kylie was the part that was going in his favor. "First off, the wedding and Kylie. Two separate things, never again to be talked about in the same discussion. Me agreeing to this wedding has no standing on my decisions about Kylie's life."

"Got it," Gage said, forgetting how sexy Darcy looked when she was ticked. And the offer had more than ticked her off, it had riled her up.

"As for the wedding, I can't believe you'd think I'd consider that offer."

"I knew it would offend you." Gage smiled, wondering why it was so important that he'd been right.

"Then why did you send it?"

"Because my brothers wouldn't shut up about more money until you shot them down." And he would always have a small question burning in his gut, a curiosity that would be impossible to ignore. The past five years had taught him that. "I'd be happy to relay any message you have to them."

"I will do the wedding here at Belle Mont House." She stood and walked over to a small desk in the corner of the kitchen and grabbed a contract. "Rhett and Stephanie will have access to all of the approved vendors on my list. And any area that I don't have covered, such as security, they can select their own company."

"Should I be taking notes?"

"I already have a new contract made up."

"Of course you do." He smiled when she walked over to a small desk in the corner of the kitchen and grabbed a contract.

"As for the planner." She slid the papers across the table. "I have put in there that I will be the exclusive designer and coordinator for the Stone and Easton wedding, but on the evening of the actual event, my assistant will run the show." She folded her hands on the table. "I'm as eager to see your mother as she is to see me, so this seemed like the best solution for everyone involved."

"It's an extremely generous option," Gage said softly, knowing that coming to that decision must have been hard for her. Agreeing to hold Rhett's wedding in her backyard was one thing, handing over the reins to her business for an event that could put Belle Mont on the map would be difficult. "Will you be here at all?"

"I will plan everything up until the rehearsal dinner, then Kylie and I are going to Disneyland, which you will see is written in the contract." He watched her flip to the third page and point at the coordinating section, but he was too busy wondering why he was unsettled by her proposed absence. "Not the actual location, but I will be charging a relocation fee for the inconvenience. But if you flip to the next page you will see that I have dropped my planner fee significantly."

He did flip the page. And that smile of his grew. "It's your normal hourly rate."

"It is."

"That's a no to the extra hundred grand then?" he asked, and she lifted a single brow. "Right. That was the offensive part."

"That's my final offer, no changes or negotiations. That is what I am willing to provide, and what I am willing to offer. If they're okay with it, I can set up a consultation and cake tasting for later this week, maybe Friday, since we are short on time. If my rules don't fit within their idea of the perfect wedding, then *we* aren't a fit."

Gage closed the contract and rested his elbows on the table. "Wow, this is a bossy place."

"It's my place, Gage," she said with the steel velvet to her voice that always managed to turn him on. "My rules. And renting Belle Mont for a night doesn't change that."

There were so many emotions packed into those words—anger, frustration, and a hint of a lingering heartache that had his chest slowly turning over.

Gage reached across the table and put his hand next to hers. He didn't cover it, just got close enough so that he could brush her fingers. Even that brief contact ignited a spark that lit up his nerve endings. Darcy's breath caught and her eyes dilated to *oh my*.

She felt the pull, and she seemed about as thrilled with the discovery as he'd been.

Interesting.

"No one is going to come in and shake things up, Pink," he assured her. And in case she was worried about what was happening between the two of them, of his intentions, he added, "You have my word. I don't want to make things any harder on either of us, I just want to move forward with my life."

"Me too," she said, a hint of naked vulnerability in her voice that kicked every one of his protective instincts into overdrive. "You have no idea how much I've wanted to do that since the wedding. And hearing you say that, knowing you want to move past it all too, makes talking about Kylie easier."

He wanted to tell her everything would be okay, that together they'd get through this, but he'd said that before. And he was done making promises he couldn't keep. Especially to Darcy.

It was clear she felt alone in all of this. A place Gage could connect with. He'd felt alone ever since Kyle passed. Standing in the middle of downtown, hanging with his friends at Stout, even surrounded by his family, there were times Gage felt the loneliness so deep it was a physical ache.

"There isn't anything you can't tell me," he said.

With a wistful smile, she linked their fingers enough to give a gentle squeeze.

Just like old times, he thought.

"Thank you," she whispered. "I've thought about this a lot, nonstop actually, and I want to do what is best for everyone involved."

"Are you saying you're open to us being a part of Kylie's life?" He couldn't help but sound hopeful.

"I'm open to you two getting to know each other."

"What does that mean?"

"Honestly, I don't even know," she said, and the look of genuine distress twisted his gut into knots. "I never really got past the part in my head where I tell you that you have a niece. I know there are things I want for her and things I won't stand to have her go through. Which is why I was thinking we'd start out slow, maybe meet at the park, see how it goes and take it from there."

"That's fair," he said, trying to curb all of the questions that were demanding to be answered. He knew how Darcy's mind worked. It started with worst case scenario and worked backwards. It was a leftover reaction to her unpredictable childhood.

Gage could attribute every successful negotiation he'd had to his ability to cut through the BS and zero in on what was important. And right then, the only thing that mattered was Kylie's future.

And his family's role in it.

He'd do whatever it took to secure that. Even if it meant using his history with Darcy to his benefit. Darcy was logical and functioned by making lists and charts, and eliminating potential problems.

Gage snagged a composition book that was on the windowsill behind him and opened to the first blank page. "Why don't we start with what you're comfortable with."

"You."

"Me?"

"Yes."

He wrote down his name, then looked up for more direction. But she remained silent, her big brown eyes wide and almost lost. He couldn't fathom the Queen of Lists only having one item on it. "Anything else to add?"

"Dogs." She bit her lip and slowly shrugged, as if saying, that's all she's got.

"Okay. Me and dogs." He flipped the page. "How about we move to things you're uncomfortable with and we can circle back to this when you're warmed up?"

"Good idea." She sat up straight. "Kylie being unsupervised. Kylie getting hurt. Kylie becoming confused over the situation." She looked down at his hand, which was not moving, and frowned. "Shouldn't you write that down?"

"Unsupervised, hurt, confused." He jotted them down. "Anything else?"

"Yes." She held up a finger. "Someone bad mouthing me or her father to Kylie. Someone lying to me about Kylie or lying to Kylie about me." Two more fingers ticked off the items. "Sleepovers, which I guess goes under unsupervised, but put it down anyway. Riding in the front seat, anything less than SPF 100 or with red dye number five in it, riding a bike—"

"Like a motorcycle?" he asked, wanting to hug her when her forehead puckered with intense concentration.

"I was thinking a pedal bike, but it would be wise to put down both," she said. "Those fruit chewies that all the kids want but keep choking on, hot dogs, and rules that defy my rules."

Gage waited for her to stop, wisely hiding his chuckle as she listed her concerns. "So no riding bikes through the park while eating licorice or fruit chewies. Anything else you're uncomfortable having around Kylie?"

"Yes," she said, her voice so full of concern he felt his chest tighten. Because her concern wasn't about Kylie right then—it was aimed at him. "The rest of your family."

Chapter Seven

G age was the glue that held his family together—it was why she hated to put him in this situation. But she'd taken Jillian's advice to heart, and didn't want there to be any misunderstandings when it came to Kylie's happiness.

"So you want Kylie to get to know us, but we can't spend time with her?" Gage asked, his voice calm and terrifyingly controlled. "Explain how you expect that to work."

"I want Kylie to spend time getting to know *you*," she clarified. "Not the defender of the Eastons, or the smooth talking negotiations expert." She waved a hand to encompass his slick tie and coat. "But the guy who wrote me that letter. The guy who's sweet and thoughtful and I know I can count on. The guy you said you wished you'd been. That's who Kylie deserves to have in her life, and that's who makes me comfortable."

"Darcy," he said, and this time he took her hand, making her more than aware of how long it had been since she'd held a man's hand. It felt good. Safe and warm. "I want to be that guy. For Kylie and for you. But she's Kyle's daughter and my family deserves to know her too."

"Being family doesn't give you automatic rights to someone's world," Darcy pointed out. "It is a position that has to be earned and respected. I'm not saying that I'm not open to eventually everyone meeting, later on down the road, but for now I want Kylie to meet the one uncle of hers that I know will keep her wellbeing at the forefront."

Here came the part that had been stressing Darcy out. The one thing that she knew would play on all of her insecurities, the reason she'd wanted a little warning before she met with Gage. Darcy knew how deeply it hurt to be abandoned, how unsettling and scary it was to have strangers coming into your home suddenly, and she refused to let her daughter experience that kind of instability. If that made her come off as a snarling mama bear, she was okay with that.

"I think the hardest person for me to become comfortable with Kylie knowing is your mom."

Gage let out a pent up breath. "I agree taking it slow is the best for Kylie, and my brothers would agree, but letting us all get to know her and leaving my mom out of it? That's going to be rough, and you know it."

"If it was just about me, I wouldn't care. But after how your mom treated me, I can't gauge how she'll react to this. So, I'm not comfortable with her meeting Kylie until I know that she won't do anything to make Kylie upset."

He was quiet for a long moment, imploring her with his eyes to change her mind. Finally, he walked to the window to stare out at the rose garden. Even from the distance, she could feel the emotions building and turning inside him.

He wanted to say her demands were unacceptable, that he'd hurt his loved ones. He looked lost and ready to run, and she almost offered him the out. Told him that as long as he promised to keep Margo in check, she could meet Kylie. She could handle Margo's snide remarks, as long as Kylie didn't have to.

But she knew from experience that no one could keep Margo in check. And opening Kylie up to that kind of censure wasn't a possibility.

Darcy stood too, going to stand beside him. They remained silent while watching Fancy prance around and entertain the Heirloom Bloomers.

"You're asking me to tell my mom she has a grandchild, but she has to wait to meet her?" He stared blindly out the window. "She's going to be crushed."

Darcy's firsthand experience with how Margo behaved when she was crushed was reason enough for her caution.

"I know how hard it will be," she said, then waited for him to turn her way, and when he did the torn look in his eyes was enough to floor her.

"But this isn't about Margo's timeline, or even mine. This is about Kylie, and when *she's* ready to meet everyone."

Friday afternoon, Darcy lugged the picnic basket out of the truck, her body rebelling from what felt like an endless week. She'd spent the first half of it obsessing over Gage changing his mind, and when he didn't call to cancel—or confirm—she distracted herself by eating her way through a batch of Jillian's tester cakes. Vanilla bean cake with mango mousse frosting—the star for tonight's scheduled cake tasting. And the reason her dress fit so tightly.

That Gage was scheduled to meet them here, at West Hills Duck Pond, only made it worse. The sun was high, there were a few scattered clouds overhead, and all of the flowers were in full bloom, making the main strip of town a shopper's utopia.

She had been stubborn the other day, offering her demands and leaving no wiggle room. But she knew better than to cut an Easton any slack. You give an inch and they walk away with everything you hold dear.

"Did you remember to bring the duckies' bread?" Kylie asked.

"It's in the picnic basket." Darcy unstrapped Kylie from the back seat. "Did you remember your windbreaker in case it starts sprinkling?"

"Ah huh. I brought a pillow too," she said, clutching a small blue and white polka dotted beanbag from one of her tossing games. "For his doggie."

Darcy took a deep breath and cupped her daughter's cheek. They'd been over this a dozen times already that morning. "I don't know if Gage is bringing the dog." She wasn't even sure he'd show at this point. "But no matter what, you and I are going to have a great time. We'll picnic, play on the swings, and feed the ducks."

"Don't worry, Mommy, today will be perfect, just like you said." Kylie patted Darcy's hand in a maternal way that made Darcy wonder just how transparent her emotions were if a four-year-old could detect them. "See, Mister's already here."

Darcy's stomach fluttered over the awareness of his presence—and that worried her.

This is a mistake, she told herself. The wedding, today, the whole thing was a recipe for heartbreak. Yet, she couldn't imagine turning back.

She peeked over the hood of her car and suddenly her nerves quelled. The fear faded, and her world spun back to safe. Because under an oak tree, sitting on a park bench, looking calm and confident—like the safe harbor she'd been searching for—was Gage.

Today, the slick sales guy had traded in the slacks for a pair of worn blue jeans, a rock band tee, and a day's worth of scruff. He looked warm and approachable, and like he'd really listened to her concerns and, most importantly, taken them to heart.

But what had her releasing a warm sigh was a ball cap. A simple, faded ball cap that was pulled low, the bill curved like he'd been worrying it with his palm. Darcy had given it to him on his birthday, years ago.

He hadn't tossed it or burned it. He'd kept it, and that had to mean something. Something that gave her hope she'd made the right decision, and today would indeed be perfect.

"That he is," Darcy said with a smile, helping Kylie out of the car. She took her hands as they crossed the street.

"Do you think he knows how to twirl?" Kylie whispered, her voice animated with excitement. "'Cuz I brought my veil, just in case he wants to learn. Sometimes a twirl comes in handy."

Darcy bit back a smile. "That was smart of you. You never know when you'll need a veil."

Kylie stepped up on the curb and then paused to look back wistfully at the car. "I should have brought my tutu."

Darcy wasn't the only one struggling with nerves. Ever since she'd explained that Gage was her uncle, Kylie had been looking through her Daddy Photo Album, and asking all kinds of questions. Where Gage lived, how old his dog was, if he was free for Christmas dinner, and if he liked cake as much as they did.

With Darcy's dad unknown, and her mom passing before Kylie was born, her daughter had never met any relatives. Which wasn't necessarily a bad thing, because it also meant that Kylie didn't know deep disappointment.

Darcy had made a wonderful group of friends, who'd rallied around them, but at holiday time it was always just Kylie and Darcy. Which had been enough for Darcy, but it was clear that Kylie was ready to expand their circle.

"Maybe next time," Darcy said optimistically, hoping for Kylie's sake there would be a next time.

"He brought the dog," Kylie squealed, dropping Darcy's hand so she could wave the beanbag excitedly at the white ball of excitement. Fancy took one look at the "pillow" and went bridezilla, barking and tugging at his leash to get free—and get the pillow.

"He likes it! He likes it!" Kylie tugged on Darcy's dress, which was cute enough for this monumental day, but not so dressy that it gave off a business vibe. This afternoon was about Kylie, about making friendships, not the wedding.

In fact, Darcy had told Gage to have Stephanie or Rhett contact her about the wedding. It was her way of keeping things simple. Making sure one relationship didn't interfere with the forward momentum of the other. Now that she'd decided to let Kylie and Gage meet, Darcy was committed to making this work. And introducing the elevated emotions of a wedding into an already fragile situation wasn't a smart move.

Darcy was determined to be smart about this, so she'd broken up the day. A quiet afternoon at the park with Gage and Kylie, then a late cake tasting with the couple of the hour back at Belle Mont House.

"I see that," Darcy said. "Why don't you run over and say hi. His name is Fancy."

"Fancy!" Kylie's feet picked up pace the second they hit the grass. She didn't slow down until she was sitting on the bench with the dog in her lap. "Mommy said you might bring Fancy, so I brought this to play fetch. Does he play fetch? Because our old neighbor Ms. Kent had a dog and he didn't like to play, but he was okay with pets. Does Fancy like pets?" Kylie said in one long breath with no pauses, her voice elevating with each word.

Gage sat speechless, taking in hurricane Kylie, with a look of complete shock. Maybe awe was a better word, because beneath the amazement was so much adoration Darcy could feel it. He was taking an inventory, putting every single feature and moment to memory, storing it for a rainy day.

"Mister?" Kylie turned those baby blues Gage's way. "Did you hear me?"

"Yeah Tiny, I heard you." He reached out to ruffle Kylie's hair, but his gaze landed on Darcy—heartfelt and full of gratitude. "And I don't know. He's not my dog, he belongs to a friend. But I do know that he likes to play dress up."

"I like to play dress up too!"

"I figured. So, instead of getting Fancy dressed, I brought along all of his clothes. Maybe you could help me get him ready?"

"Do you have a tutu?"

"You know what, I just might." Gage opened his briefcase, and instead of contracts and files, it was filled with dog clothes. Feminine, frilly, couture critter wear that put Darcy's dress to shame. "Take a look in there and see if there isn't something you like."

"There's a higher chance that we'll be here all day while she puts Fancy in each and every one that she *does* like," Darcy laughed. "That Marry Poppins briefcase of yours is every little girl's fantasy for dress up."

"Does that apply to mothers of little girls, too?"

"What?" Darcy jerked her gaze north, away from the way his soft tee stretched across his chest.

Not that staring at his lips was any better, but that's where her gaze hung. She'd like to think it was because he was smiling, but she had a feeling it had more to do with how kissable that smile was.

"Dress up?" he said. "Is that a mother's fantasy too?"

"Wouldn't you like to know."

"Actually, I would. So that next time I can bring something for you too." His grin widened. "Just trying to be a gentleman."

"Gentlemen bring flowers," she said quite primly. Then she turned her attention to the reason for their picnic. "What did you find?"

"A raincoat, a hoodie, and, oh look, a snow hat." Bubbling with excitement, she turned to Gage. "Can we stay until I try them all on Fancy?"

"I'm not in any rush," Gage said, looking at Darcy for direction.

For a fleeting moment, it was as if they were a family enjoying a day at the park. With Kylie asking for a full day of fun, Gage looking up at her as if there was nowhere else he'd rather be, and Darcy feeling as if she wasn't in this alone.

An expert would probably tell her it was that Gage was Kyle's twin, but Darcy knew it was more than that. She'd never felt like Kyle was on her team. Even when they'd discovered she was pregnant, Kyle didn't give them the kind of focus and devotion their relationship needed. He didn't give Darcy the love she deserved.

Gage had always been different. Grounded to Kyle's ever-changing world, favoring insightfulness over charisma. Had Gage been single when they'd met, or Darcy's mom hadn't only passed when she'd started dating Kyle, maybe it would have turned out differently.

But things for Kylie would be different.

"I don't have to be back until four, so I guess it's a fashion show day in the park," Darcy said.

"Let's get styling," Gage said, taking a seat on the grass with Fancy, and bringing the suitcase with him so it would be easier on Kylie.

Heart in her throat, Darcy busied herself with setting out lunch, careful to pick a table far enough away so as not to interrupt the bonding that was transpiring over doggie fashion. After a few moments, Gage and Kylie stood over what appeared to be enough clothes to fill Kim Kardashian's closet.

Fancy was wearing a yellow rain coat with a matching hat and galoshes. The other two sat knee to knee, the collection spread out between them.

Kylie placed a tiara on Fancy's head. "I still don't see a tutu."

"Let me see if it's at the bottom." Gage dumped out the contents of the briefcase. A genie's hat, mini-Ugg boots, and a Burberry coat fell to the grass. "Three different colored boas, but no tutu."

"How about this?" Kylie asked, slipping a blue ruffled headband around Fancy's head, unable to get it passed his neck.

"I got an idea," he said, undoing his shoe. "Pick out one of the boas. I bet we can make it into a tutu."

Kylie picked up each of the boas, silently debating which color would be the best. Darcy could tell she wanted the lavender one, but kept going back to the blue one, as if afraid that if she picked too girly of a color the fun day would end. Tongue peeking out, she settled on the lavender one, then handed it over to Gage.

"Excellent choice," he said and Kylie beamed at the praise. "It matches these."

Gage held up a pair of lavender booties, which he'd stuck on his fingers, and began moving them across the lawn. Fancy barked with excitement, and Kylie giggled so hard she fell over.

"But we still don't got a tutu," Kylie said, batting those lashes Gage's way. She had his number. And, man oh man, he had hers.

"Ah, be prepared to be amazed, little lady."

"I like it when you call me Tiny," Kylie interrupted.

He glanced at Kylie and grinned. "Got it. But if I call you Tiny, then how about you call me Gage?"

Kylie cocked her head, her expression one of deep contemplation. "I like Mister a lot, you looked like a Mister the other day." Kylie stood, getting eye level with Gage and took off his ball cap. She styled his hair, making more of a mess than anything, then put the hat back on. "But you don't look like a Mister now."

Darcy snickered and Gage sent her a sidelong look in warning. "Do I look like a Gage?"

Lips pursed in concentration, Kylie walked slowly around Gage, sizing him up, her fingers poking him in the cheek, the neck, the back of his shoulder. And when she completed the circle, she got down on her knees and put both hands on his cheeks.

Turning his head from one side to the other, she finally sat back. "You look like my daddy, but Mommy said I can't call you that, 'cuz only my daddy's my daddy. She said I can call you Gage, or Uncle Gage or Mister. I got to choose."

Emotions clouded Darcy's eyes as she watched Gage struggle to hold it together. His throat worked hard, his breath came in sharp bursts, and his face radiated with thankfulness. "Your mom's right, even though I look like your daddy, I'm not. He was my brother. Which makes me your uncle."

Kylie's arms went wide a second before she launched herself into Gage's arms and wrapped herself around him like a monkey. "I've never had an uncle before."

Gage didn't waste a moment, scooping Kylie up into his arms and holding her tight. His eyes closed and Darcy watched him bury his head in Kylie's hair, and she knew what he was doing.

She did it every time she needed a reminder of how wonderful life could be. He was breathing in the scent of heaven. Pure and sweet and so powerful it had the ability to wash away even the deepest aches.

"I've never been an uncle before, so that makes us a perfect pair." Gage looked over the top of Kylie's caramel curls and mouthed, *Thank you.*

"You know what?" Kylie leaned back. "Sam's uncle buys him ice cream *before* dinner and even lets him get sprinkles. And one time he let Sam stay up way past bedtime to play video games, and didn't even make him brush his teeth."

Gage laughed, rough and low. "Well, I don't know about all of that, but I can show you how to make a tutu out of a boa and a shoelace. In fact, one shoelace and Fancy will be twirling around the lawn like a prima ballerina."

He loosened one from his shoe, then waited for Kylie to pull it out, making a slithering sound when she did. Kylie, completely smitten at this point, giggled as he wove it through the seam of the boa, gathering it as he went. In a matter of seconds, he'd transformed the boa into a big, fluffy tutu. And himself from estranged uncle to Kylie's own personal hero.

"How's that?" he asked.

"Perfect!" she shrieked, looking wide eyed at Gage as if he'd announced he'd invented cake. "Isn't it perfect, Mommy? We did it!"

Gage looked up and gave a boyish smile, so similar to Kyle's her pulse galloped. But instead of that smile telling her he had it, Gage's grin was asking her how he was doing. That he was trying to earn her trust spoke volumes, that he was being so patient and gentle with Kylie brought tears to her eyes.

"Perfect," she said, because she couldn't think of a better word.

His gaze locked on hers, so intense, yet so gentle she found herself holding her breath. Being on the receiving end of that kind of focus was overwhelming, exciting even. She felt as though he was seeing every inch of the real her, taking in the reality of what their life was like—and he was drawn in.

"Pretty dang perfect," he said, and although Darcy told herself he was talking about his time with Kylie, she couldn't help but notice that his focus had dropped to her lips.

Looking away before the heat covered her cheeks, Darcy went back to setting up lunch, ignoring the tingling in her stomach. She hadn't tingled since Kyle. And to tingle now, like this, over his twin, didn't seem right.

But when she looked back over her shoulder again, and watched Gage lift Kylie on his lap to demonstrated how to tie a knot, she decided not to ignore the tingles. At least for today. Because this is what she wanted for Kylie. This moment, right here.

Laughter. Family. Connection.

Happiness.

And no matter how hard it got, she would do anything to keep her kid as happy as she was right then.

And what about your happiness, her heart whispered, because Kylie wasn't the only one who was in danger of becoming smitten.

Gage sat in his car and watched Darcy's taillights disappear down the street, and he wished Darcy had slowed down long enough for them to say more than a few passing words. Not that he'd minded watching her flit around in that dress.

Closing his eyes, he could still picture it. Cream, with light pink flowers that matched her lips, the soft fabric rippling against her body when she moved. He could especially picture the way it had flirted around her knees when she sat—never next to him, but as far away as the table would allow.

It was if she'd been on the periphery of the afternoon, watching and observing, but never engaging. Oh, she'd been there for Kylie, attentive and open, but had kept him at a distance. He'd caught her watching him from afar a few times, but before he could wave her over, she'd go back to writing in her journal.

She'd given him everything he'd wanted today to be—but nothing of herself. And that left him wanting.

For the past week, he'd been looking forward to today, even avoided contact as not to give Darcy an opportunity to cancel. And while he appreciated the time alone to get to know Kylie, he wanted to get to know Darcy again.

Strangely enough, seeing her in the mother role hadn't been the visual confirmation to back the fuck off that he'd hoped it would be. Instead, he was completely captivated. Watching her with Kylie, the way she confidently ran her business, only confirmed that she had grown into the incredible woman he knew she would.

What was wrong with Kyle that he let her get away? And how could he, knowing what his future held, throw it all away on a drinking induced tantrum? Women like Darcy came along once in a lifetime, and he'd bet no one had ever told her that.

And now she was heading home, for a wedding consultation, and he hadn't even had the chance to tell her how impressed he was with her. What a great mom she was, and how she'd managed to raise one hell of a great kid.

Sliding his leather jacket on, he transformed from Uncle Gage back into, what had Darcy called it?

Oh yeah, the smooth talking negotiations expert.

"Thanks for taking one for the team," he said to his passenger, who looked like he deserved a stage name—and he wasn't talking Broadway. "And extra treats for not going for a doggie high five to the crotch. Your restraint was impressive."

"Yip!"

Gage stuck his fist out and Fancy nose bumped it. Window cracked, he started the car and he and the Dog Wonder-ful headed up Main Street. Fresh air blew through the car, bring with it the scent of earthy pine and summer days at his dad's cabin.

A quieting peace from the day settled over him as he wound through streets that were older than the city, columned brick houses and bright-colored Victorians that spoke of another era flying past. Fancy leaned against the door, his head stuck out the window, his ears blowing back as he too enjoyed the leisurely drive up West Hills.

Gage wasn't in any hurry, he had plenty of time before his meeting started, so he stared out the window and replayed the moment when Kylie had called him Uncle Gage. Over and over until his smile was so big he was sure he looked like a fool. Not that he cared. Uncles were allowed to make fools of themselves.

Something he reminded himself of moments later, when he saw the familiar brick driveway and pulled in, reaching the end of the road and parking next to the cottage—just as Darcy was rushing out of her house and across the rose garden.

She'd changed her clothes. Gone was the cute summer dress from earlier that was soft, hit above the knees, and clung to the right places. In its place was one of those power dresses she favored so much. This one was navy blue on the bottom, hugging those legs and hips, white up top, cinched with a belt in the middle to show off her tiny waist. And don't even get him started on the buttons. They began at the neckline and went all way down the front.

And she left the top two undone enough that when she reached the driveway and leaned down to see who was in the car, he got enough of a view of white lace and creamy cleavage to have him manning up below the belt.

But when he saw the pink tint on her nose from a day in the sun, and her hair, which had blown loose from those up-dos she wore, he knew he was toast. He wanted her—more than was safe.

She was staring at him, too—squinting to be exact— as if she could get her eyes narrow enough he'd morph into anyone other than him.

Gage hopped out of the car, Stephanie's wedding book in hand, and smiled. "I'm a few minutes early."

"I would ask what you're doing here," she said tartly. "But that seems to be a redundant question at this point."

"I'm here for our new client appointment." He handed her Rhett's signed contract.

"Rhett and Stephanie are my new clients. Not you."

"Rhett is out of town." He leaned in, close enough to see the pulse in her neck beat. "Where's Kylie?"

"Taking a nap. She was having too much fun, and skipped her afternoon nap to play doggie dress up at the park."

"I heard she was with her uncle." Gage straightened and leaned his hip against the front of his car. "Guy must be a total douche for letting her miss naptime. I hope he at least said thank you."

She didn't smile, but her lips twitched at the corners and her eyes lit with humor. "I'm sorry Rhett will miss this, but Stephanie will be here in a few minutes, and I need to get prepared."

"Stephanie's not coming." And neither was Kylie, which meant they were alone. "And you look more than ready."

She dusted her hands down the front of her dress, then reached for her hair. "I look like a mommy who spent the day at a windy park chasing a dog."

Gage reached out slowly, giving her time to step away. When she didn't, he tucked a strand of hair that had escaped behind her ear. "You look beautiful."

His voice fell to a whisper because touching her skin made it difficult to breathe. He hadn't touched her like this since before Kyle had made his intentions clear. He forgot how smooth she felt, how soft.

"Thank you." He let his hand slowly fall away. "For raising an amazing kid, for giving me today, and for letting her miss her naptime. What you've created here is special." Gage looked to the quaint cottage, with the flower pots in the window and the makeshift dance barre on the porch. "It's magical."

"You were great with her. And Kylie deserves a little magic in her world."

"So do you."

An uncertain expression played on her face, and he could tell that she wanted to believe him, but was gun shy. After her childhood, then his family, her hesitation was understandable. Yet, it still rubbed him wrong that trust was still such a foreign concept for her.

"So you came here to say thanks?" she asked, taking a cautious step back.

"I came here to tell you that Stephanie doesn't get back until Monday, and she asked me to deliver the contract and this." He held up the four-inch binder that was comprehensive enough to plan an Inaugural Ball at the White House, and heavy enough to double as a weapon. Leaving out the part where he'd known since before their last meeting that Stephanie would be unavailable today.

"You could have told me that at the park," she called his bluff.

"I could have, but it would break rule number one, mixing business with family."

A trembling laughed escaped. "The dog. The park. That." She pointed to the binder. "You listened."

"I listen to everything you say," he said, wondering how many times she'd gone unheard. By the look on her face, he didn't even want to guess. It would ruin his good mood.

"Thank you."

"You have a big enough heart to give me a second chance. I'm not going to blow this."

He'd gone to the park with the intention of being the spokesperson for his family. But after two seconds with these two ladies, Gage knew he was in deep.

He'd somehow gone from being the defender of the Eastons to the protector of the Kincaids. Which left him torn between two families—both with different agendas.

"And you drove all this way to make sure they were kept separate?"

"Yup. I'd drive to New York and back if it meant seeing you smile like that."

"New York is a long drive for a smile." Her lips tilted up even more, shy like, as if she were liking the banter.

"That's some smile." His eyes fell to her lips, full and glossy, and damn near perfect. "And when it's aimed at me, I end up saying things that I shouldn't."

"Who said I was aiming it at you? Maybe I was just smiling and you happened to step in front of me."

"Pink, I know when you're smiling, and when you're smiling at me." He leaned in, and, in that tone that usually had women melting like putty, said, "there's a difference."

"Why do you insist on calling me Pink? I never wear pink."

He grinned. "You did that first day I met you."

"I wore a blue top."

"I wasn't commenting on the color of your top." When she didn't even blink, he flashed his trademark grin, the one that had been passed down from Easton father to Easton son. "That black skirt of yours was awfully short, and when you bent over to grab my pencil for me..."

Her mouth gaped open. "You dropped it like five times."

"Seven," he said, remembering every single time.

"Men." She snorted. And although her expression gave nothing away, he could tell she felt it. That undeniable heat that went from zero to surface-of-the-sun whenever they were within sparing distance.

"But if you don't like Pink, I can always come up with something different." Gage held his car keys out and made a big show of dropping them. "Whoops, look at that, I dropped my keys and I can't get them because my hands are full."

She took the wedding album and gave a *that's the best you got?* smile.

"Hey, it worked before." He picked up the keys. "Now, how about we go inside and get to that meeting of ours?"

"Right. Explain to me again why the woman, whose wedding was so important I had to uproot my life, couldn't make a mandatory meeting, which she agreed to?" Darcy asked warily.

"It's just this meeting," Gage said. "And I offered to drop off the contract and her book, which, if you flip through, you'll see the woman has dedicated a good ten thousand hours to planning the perfect day."

Darcy opened the book, and with a glare that could have blistered paint, flipped to the first page—which Gage still didn't understand. It was sketches of hair styles, rudimentary and definitely old fashioned. It made no sense. But Miss Planner didn't bat an eye, just mumbled, "interesting," and flipped to the next page.

Which was even more confusing. Pictures of wedding tents, cut from magazines, not a single one of them even remotely similar. To everyone else they would look like a jumble of ideas and fabric swatches, but to Darcy they must have made sense, because she looked up and said, "She has a very clear idea of what she wants."

"You got all of that from magazine pages and stick figures?"

"Just like you can read a contract and know what everyone's really looking for in the deal, I can look at these pictures and decipher what Stephanie really wants."

Gage looked over her shoulder at a photo that showed some kind of giant circus tent, with dozens of white branched trees covered in twinkle lights, and silver globes hanging from the ceiling. "What, a stuffy wedding?"

"No, to feel cherished." Darcy's eyes lit with warmth and yearning, and those instincts that had caused Gage trouble in the past, kicked in. He wanted to tell her she deserved to be cherished too, but before he could say a word, she was closing the book and looking antsy. "I'll study these and give her a call on Monday. That will give me a chance to put a presentation together."

Gage shoved his hands in his pockets. "So, that's it?"

Darcy looked at Fancy, who was standing on the dashboard, making a picture with his tongue on the front windshield. "That's it."

"Then I guess I should get going."

"I should probably get back to the cottage. It's Finger Food Friday, and Kylie likes to help with the preparation. Even though I think it's more about the chef's costume."

Gage smiled at the image of Tiny in an apron and chef's hat. Darcy lowered her lashes, and—*holy Christ*—that loose piece of hair escaped, falling softly across her cheek, and suddenly, all he could picture was Darcy. Standing in her kitchen in an apron, those heels from the other day—and nothing else. And it took everything he had to keep his eyes from straying to places he had no business straying.

Not that it mattered, the air turned charged and he watched as Darcy's pulse picked up at the base of her neck—because, yeah, he'd strayed, and she was stunning.

And every single one of the million and three reasons he'd listed over the years, of why *not* to go there, vanished. Because Gage might not know the best way to handle this situation, but he knew women. And Darcy's thoughts weren't that far off from his.

"I didn't expect this to be so—" she swallowed, "—intimate."

"Me either. But I should have expected it."

As if afraid to ask him what *that* meant, she said, "No, I bet it's just spending the day together, with Kylie, then talking about wedding stuff. They're the two things in my life that I feel passionately about. And sharing them with you, like this, feels…"

"Intimate."

"Yeah."

Neither of them moved, to leave or to get closer. They just stood there, staring, as if they were both seeing each other with fresh eyes. Eyes that weren't clouded with history or anger or judgment. And when the newness turned to interest, and the interest to something heavier, finally Gage took a step back.

"Good night, Pink," he said, taking another step. Then two more.

"Wait." Darcy took a step, then stopped. "What about the cake tasting? Jillian, my friend, she owns Cake Goddess, she has a special tasting ready in the main house. She needs time to design it, and designs are determined by flavor composition." She waved a nervous hand. "I don't know much about it really, it's her thing. But she assures me it's an important step in the process, and she needs to know what flavor combination, or combinations, Stephanie and Rhett want for their wedding. And she's already behind, and it's important."

"You already said that." Gage thought about walking inside that house and taking a seat at the table. Not the one in the main house, but Darcy's house. The cottage with the family ready porch and the welcoming front door. Then he thought about how much trouble they could get into making finger foods, and then he was staring at her lips.

Again.

She had an amazing mouth. Full and lush and sweet.

So damn sweet he found himself unable to tear his gaze away, and instead of moving backward and diffusing the building heat, he took a step forward and threw some gasoline on that fire.

"Gage," she breathed, and he could almost taste the strawberries from lunch on her lips. "Do you want to come and sample the cakes? It's an important part of the process."

"Is that the Cake Goddess's thing or yours?"

"It's my thing, I guess." Her eyes fluttered up and—*bam*—he was a goner. Somehow transported back to junior year, when she aced her final.

They stayed up all night in his room, studying, because she was afraid she'd fail. So when the professor posted their grades, he was right there and she wrapped those arms around his neck and gave him a hug that had him questioning everything. Then she looked up at him with those soul-melting eyes and he'd damn near kissed her.

Even though he'd been dating Cheryl.

And instead of saying, *Fuck yeah, he was down for a tasting,* he heard himself say, "I'll have to take a raincheck. I have dinner with my brothers."

And just like seven years ago, Darcy took a big step back and worried the fabric of her dress.

"Right, Friday night family dinners," she said with a jerky laugh, and that smile went from playful to professional. But there was a wistful tone that made him think she missed family dinners.

Darcy hadn't just opened her heart to Kyle, she opened it to the entire Easton clan. Even Margo. She'd been to family dinners, reunions, every important event since Kyle had first brought her home. They'd become her family, and she'd become theirs. Up until the wedding they'd been her entire world—and she'd been cut off without even an explanation.

That kind of loss would wreck the strongest of people, yet Darcy had managed to pull her world back together. Make her own family out of the wreckage.

Gage considered asking her to come, but then he'd have to explain it was at his mom's house. And look at that, one thought of his mom and Gage's body temperature went from heated interest to stone cold—sending his boys into hiding.

He must have been quiet for too long, because her smile cracked at the edges and she said, "I can use the cake for a tasting I have tomorrow, no biggie."

"If time is an issue, I think I saw a picture of a cake Stephanie was going on and on about on her Pinterest wall. Something about Princess Kate, and gold leafing. You'll see it." He turned to open his door, but bumped into it instead. "You and the Cake Goddess can decide what kind of cake would work best. As long as it isn't chocolate, it should be fine." And then, because he couldn't seem to shut up, he added, "You know, Rhett hates chocolate."

"I remembered. Say hi to everyone for me…Never mind." Shaking her head, she wrapped her arms around herself in a protective move. "Forget I said that. Have a good night, Gage."

Chapter Eight

He was being watched.

Gage felt it with every fiber of his being. His body ached as if he'd managed less than a few hours of sleep, and the hot doggy breath on his neck was saying that was all he was going to get.

Littleshit wanted to be fed.

"We're in a standoff, pal," Gage said, rolling on his back and putting the pillow over his face. "You're hungry and I'm exhausted. Maybe if you didn't keep me up all night with that whining, I wouldn't feel the need to sleep past breakfast."

Fancy laid down on Gage's chest and let out a pathetic whimper. Gage sighed in defeat and eyed the dog. "For a guy who tries to rip people's fingers off, you sure are needy."

"Yip."

"Breakfast. Yeah, I got it when you dragged your bowl in here an hour ago and started acting like I starve you." Gage tossed back the covers and sat up, his eyes scratchy and irritated.

With a glare that said he wasn't happy about this arrangement, Gage tucked the dog under his arm like a football and padded to the kitchen.

Fancy panted happily, turning those big wet doggie eyes up at Gage. His expression full of gleeful innocence—as if this hadn't been *his* plan.

"Don't get comfortable," Gage said, as he glanced at the clock over the fireplace. It wasn't even seven. On Saturday morning. Better than dawn, but not as good as nine-thirty. "One more night, then you go back where you belong, and I get to sleep more than three hours without taking a potty walk."

Fancy whimpered his apology. Potty walks when one lived in a downtown high-rise meant more than just opening the back door in your underwear.

"Nothing personal, I just don't share my bed with dogs. And if I did, he'd be a big beast of a thing, with a spiked collar, and jowls, who didn't force me to put silk sheets on the bed."

This time his yip sounded more like a defensive yap. And there were definitely teeth involved.

Gage jerked his hand out of bite range. "Hey, all I'm saying is for that much trouble, there had better be a naked woman waiting for me in those sheets."

So what if the woman he imagined looked a hell of a lot like Darcy, right down to the melt-your-soul eyes and mile-long legs—which would be wearing nothing but a thong and tanned legs in those sheets. If he was showing off his silk, it was only fair she showed off hers.

"Any sane woman would take one look at the state of this kitchen and you'd never get her into the bedroom."

Margo Easton sat at his kitchen table in a charcoal grey suit, heels, and enough diamonds to accessorize the Grammys, serenely sipping coffee—and folding his clean clothes.

"I was going to fold those." Gage scowled down at Littleshit, whose nose was tucked securely between Gage's bicep and chest. "You could have at least warned me."

Not a single yip in response.

"What are you doing here, Mom?" Gage asked, giving her a kiss to the forehead before pulling the doggie kibble out of the pantry.

"Making my son coffee." She reached for a pair of boxer-briefs and Gage watched in horror as Margo smoothed them out with her hands, then folded them into a neat little square. "Can't a mother wake her son up with a fresh pot of coffee and folded clothes?"

Gage looked at the pot on the counter. It was empty. Next to it sat two paper cups boasting the logo from the roasting company in the lobby of his building.

"You brought coffee from downstairs," he said.

Margo took a sip from the cup she must have snagged from his cupboard. "Your coffee pot is different than mine. All those buttons and levers,

I never know what to push. Plus, it doesn't make blueberry scones. And I know you like blueberry scones."

His stomach growled on cue, which delighted Margo. "I figured that you must have been starved. Seeing as you missed family dinner last night."

And the reason for her visit, Gage thought, setting Littleshit on the floor. He grabbed a pair of folded jeans and a clean shirt still in the basket next to the table and tugged them on. Then he filled a cereal bowl with kibble and set it down. Everyone looked offended. Margo for serving a dog out of a people bowl. And the dog for getting kibble.

"You wanted the good stuff? Then next time don't leave a brother hanging," he whispered. To his mom. "Sorry I missed dinner."

"I was just worried. You haven't missed a family dinner since college." Not true. Gage hadn't missed a family dinner since Kyle died. "With no call to let me know you weren't coming, I got worried." Margo rolled his socks and set them pointedly on the table. "So here I am, with scones and coffee, checking on my boy."

Gage released a breath, the guilt so heavy he took a seat at the table. "I didn't go to dinner last night because I was dropping off wedding stuff for Rhett at Belle Mont, but I should have called."

By the time he'd arrived back at his loft, his mind was spinning. He didn't need a family dinner, he needed time to process. To figure out what kind of role he'd play in Kylie's life. In Darcy's. And how it would affect his family.

Gage was a fixer, the glue that held it all together. He'd assigned himself that role when, instead of being there for Kyle, when he'd needed his twin most, Gage had been off licking his own wounds. Trying to wrap his head around that fact that even though the wedding was canceled, Darcy would always be off limits.

This time he intended to keep his focus, and find a way to bring everyone together. Only, a week into his plan and he'd nearly botched it all. He'd been one breath away from kissing Darcy. And kissing his hard won control goodbye.

"She'll make a lovely bride. Don't you think?"

"What?" Gage looked up.

"Stephanie." Margo said exasperated. "Did you hear? Her dress is going to be made by Vera Wang, as a present. Well, of course you didn't hear, you weren't at dinner. But it's going to be lovely. And the cake, my goodness, it will be the talk for years to come. Seven tiers, gold leafing, and the Cake Goddess is making it."

"That I heard," Gage said, thinking about the way Darcy had looked, standing beneath the old oak tree in her dress, all buttoned up but nervous as she'd invited him to taste her cakes. Then he remembered how her smile faded when he told her about family dinner.

"You can bet I'm going to be at that appointment."

Gage froze. "Maybe you should let the love birds go to that one alone."

"Why would I do that?" She took another casual sip.

Littleshit glanced at the door—looking for an escape. So did Gage, but he willed himself to remain calm. There was no way she knew about Darcy. His brothers had all agreed that they'd wait until Stephanie came back to tell her the news.

"Isn't that what being engaged is about? Eating free cake and disgusting public displays of affection?" Even as he said it, he couldn't remember a single time Stephanie and Rhett had engaged in any form of PDA, other than a quick peck.

Then again, they were in the spotlight all the time. Maybe that was their way of keeping some things private.

"Well, that's a relief," Margo said. "Here I thought you were trying to keep me away from Darcy Kincaid."

Gage ran a hand down his face, his stubble rubbing as sharp as his mom's tone. "Who told you?"

His mother pressed a nonexistent seam out of a t shirt, then plucked at the sleeve. "Do you really have to ask? Last night was family dinner, and I love your brothers dearly, but they gossip more than my ladies bridge club."

So much for brotherly bonds. "We were going to tell you when Stephanie got home. We didn't want to upset you until we knew Belle Mont was completely locked down."

"Well, if it was for my own good, then who am I to complain?" she said, not looking at him directly. "I guess I should be thanking you." Clothes forgotten, she stood and walked to put her cup in the sink. "I'll be going then."

"Don't go, Mom." Gage took the cup from her hand and set it on the counter. "Let me make you some breakfast or at least share my scone while you tell me what you came here to say. Otherwise, you won't be able to sleep tonight."

Margo might be a busybody when it came to her family, but her concern originated from a good place. Usually. She was a warm and loving mom, big on hugs as encouragement when Gage had been younger. But after their dad died, her fear of loss made her distant, and the hugs turned into pats on the cheek. And when Kyle died, her interest in her sons' happiness became a mission.

One she was willing to stop at nothing to secure. Even if it meant burning bridges or driving her sons crazy in the process. And when, one by one, her boys grew up and left the nest, she began to find more creative ways to insert herself in their lives.

Such as impromptu early morning coffee chats.

"It's nothing," she said flippantly.

"If it was nothing, you wouldn't be in my kitchen at seven on my one day off."

Silence.

"Mom?" Gage leaned against the counter, showing her he had all the time in the world.

"If you must know, it's that woman! She's been back in our lives for less than a few weeks. A few weeks!" Margo's eyes were watery, but fierce. "Already the deceit and lies have begun."

Margo didn't do tears. It was an action she couldn't seem to find the energy for after losing Kyle. But she did guilt like any good Catholic mother—lovingly and with pizazz.

"No one is trying to deceive you," Gage said, pulling his mom into his arms and resting his cheek on her head. Margo might have the attitude of a rhino when riled, but she only came to Gage's chest. "Darcy was as surprised to see me as I was her when I showed up for the first meeting."

"First meeting?" Margo pulled back. "You make it sound like there was more than one."

At Gage's silence, she began pacing, her heels clicking on the slate tile as if she were giving voice to every thought racing through her mind. "Secret rendezvous! Missing members at family dinners! Outrageous demands!"

"There haven't been any rendezvouses." Although, there had been a brief moment yesterday where it had felt like exactly that. A secret rendezvous, with a special lady, that had the potential for magic. "And if anyone has issued outrageous demands, that would be me. She is letting Rhett rent the venue, working with his security team, and she even agreed to go away for the evening of the wedding."

Margo laughed. "Of course she did. The girl couldn't see a good thing through even if it was attached to her glasses."

"We don't know what all happened between them. Those were their issues, not ours," Gage said, and for the first time he didn't feel like he was betraying Kyle. He felt as if he were defending the mother of his niece. "Darcy has been more than generous."

With everything.

His mother spun around, her face pale and drawn. "There you go, already taking her side."

Jesus.

"There are no sides." Although, right then, he wasn't sure which side he'd pick. "Stephanie wants to get married at Belle Mont. Darcy owns Belle Mont. Unfortunately, for all involved, Stephanie wants to walk through the rose garden with an Easton."

Margo clutched her heart, as if Gage has personally invoked a heart attack. "Watch your mouth, Gage Matthew Easton. Stephanie is lucky to land a man like Rhett. He's successful, charming, honorable—"

"He didn't seem to mind throwing me under the bus last night at dinner."

"—loving, and voted one of the world's sexiest people."

"I'll be sure to add that to the list of things to say in my best man's speech."

She ignored this. "And Darcy should be honored to host their union. Just like she should have been honored to marry Kyle. But she always wants more."

"Whoa, Mom, let's not take this there." Because *there* is exactly where Darcy was afraid it would go. And watching his mom get all upset and red in the face, he was starting to see her point.

"I will take it wherever I like. That woman will never be happy with what she's given. It was always more, more, more." Margo shook a finger. "I blame it on her upbringing. Who could go the distance when they spent their entire formative years moving from house to house? I told her she wasn't Kyle's match, and she didn't fit within our family's character."

Gage's heart literally stopped. "Hold up, you told her that?"

He could only imagine how that must have hurt, especially since Darcy always questioned her own mother's love for her.

"Of course I told her. Why wouldn't I? She was complaining about Kyle, saying she wasn't happy." She threw her hands up. "Who couldn't be happy with a man like Kyle? After everything he'd done for her and her standing in the community, and she still wasn't happy. I chalked it up to a chemical deficiency, but Kyle had made his choice. What was a mother to do?"

"Besides making her feel inferior to the family she was supposed to be marrying into?"

Darcy must have been in a bad way if she'd gone to Margo for advice. Darcy wasn't one to talk badly of anyone, especially Kyle. It was why her actions at the wedding had been such a mystery. She'd never said boo about not being happy. And then to reach out for help, only to be shoved further under?

"Did you ask her why she was upset?"

"Oh, you know." Margo flicked her fingers dismissively. "Not enough quality time, needing to be the center of Kyle's attention, wanting different things. She said something about Kyle and his secretary, or maybe it was his intern. Who knows anymore? The point is, Kyle gave her everything, and she accused him of sneaking around."

Gage couldn't believe he was asking this, but, "Was he?"

"How would I know? I told her that Kyle wasn't raised that way. He wouldn't disgrace himself by cheating with a lowly intern. But if she was afraid something was missing in her relationship, maybe she should cut back at work and put in more effort when it came to Kyle and his needs."

"Jesus, Mom. She'd just landed a job working for the biggest event company in Portland. Her career was taking off. Why should she have to sacrifice her work when Kyle was notorious for burning the midnight oil?"

Kyle hadn't just worked late into the evenings—he'd taken work trips nearly every weekend leading up to their wedding. Darcy had grown more and more distant from him and his family during that time. Yet, Kyle had acted like everything was fine. Even at his bachelor party, he'd been all smiles and grins.

Then at the wedding, Gage remembered seeing a perky co-ed hanging around the groom's room. Later he saw her talking with Darcy, and then … that was it. Darcy was gone.

"You knew her suspicions, but you never asked if it was true?"

"Why should I?"

Gage gripped the back of his neck. "You reamed Darcy after the wedding. Had her arrested, tried to sue her, and you never thought to ask if maybe, I don't know, she called off the wedding because Kyle was cheating?"

"Even if he did stray, men cheat, Gage. Your father, God rest his soul, didn't have it in his makeup to stray. But some men do."

"No, Mom, cowards cheat. Men know what they have when they find it and hold tight."

"Kyle is dead," she said, her voice sharp enough to fillet marble. "What does it matter now?"

"Because she was pregnant. With Kyle's kid." Gage needed to sit down, but was afraid he'd be unable to get back up.

"Is that what she told you? That it's his?" Margo said, her words laced with anger. "And you believed her?"

"It's Kyle's, Mom."

"How do you know this isn't some ruse to get money from the family?"

"She hasn't asked for a penny." A weird feeling overtook him. It started low in his gut, and moved up to his chest. "Why aren't you even open to the possibility that it could be Kyle's?"

"Because Kyle didn't want kids." She said in that hoity toity, mom knows best tone that always managed to rub him wrong. "He had a career to build and he promised me he'd wait at least five years before considering kids with *her*."

"Maybe he lied."

"Gage," Margo said, sounding more hurt than horrified. "Kyle had his faults, but he wouldn't lie to me."

A few weeks ago, Gage would have sworn the same thing, but he was coming to understand that none of them really knew Kyle as well as they thought.

Tired of arguing, and not wanting to be there much longer, Gage walked into his room and grabbed his phone. When he returned, he handed it to his mother. It was opened on a picture Darcy had taken for him, of Kylie feeding the ducks. And once again, he was leveled by how much Kylie looked like Kyle—and, in turn, Gage.

"Oh my," Margo breathed, and slowly walked over to the table to sit. "She looks just like him."

Gage smiled. "Kylie has his humor too."

"Kylie. That's her name?" Margo looked up, tears glistening in her eyes. "How old is she?"

"Four, and she's a great kid."

Margo looked back at the picture. "Of course she is, she's an Easton. I can see it in the way she holds herself. So proud and diplomatic. So much like *your* father. Oh, and those curls, she is an angel." Margo focused on Gage, her smile full of a yearning so real, he felt his stomach bottom out. "When can I meet her?"

Gage took a seat and let out a breath. "Soon, I hope."

"What do you mean soon?" Margo demanded. "She is my grandchild. I want to meet her."

"And you will. Darcy just wants to make sure that we do what's best for Kylie, and I agree."

"What's best for that child is to be with her family." Margo stood, irate and determined. Not a good combination for future peace talks with Darcy. "And she can't keep me from her."

"She can." And if he couldn't get his mom to tread lightly, he had no doubt that she would.

Chapter Nine

For Darcy, a lazy Saturday morning was as rare as a fairy sighting. But with only a small vow renewal on the evening's schedule, and Kylie still sound asleep, it seemed as if the fairies were sharing some of that pixie dust.

Darcy padded out on the front porch with her sketch pad and Stephanie's wedding book. She'd spent a good portion of last night poring through her ideas, and laying out what she was sure would be Stephanie's perfect wedding.

Wanting to make a few more changes and get the layout sketched, she snuggled in the wicker swing with a hot mocha latte—extra whip. The world seemed still and quiet as the sun rose over Mount Hood. She took stock of the week and checked in with herself.

But instead of peace of mind, all of the taking stock and checking in was giving her a headache. Because without the noise and chaos of being a single mom, she was left to focus on Gage. And how she could have sworn he was about to kiss her.

Even more alarming—she would have kissed him back.

Not that anyone would have blamed her, well except his family. Spending an entire day with Gage and not thinking about a little kiss would be like a chocoholic deciding to only window shop at the local candy store.

It was his smile, she decided. Full and a little crooked, with double-barreled dimples that were as sexy as they were flirty, and a hint of kindness. They had the power to render a woman stupid. Which was exactly what she'd have been to even consider kissing Gage.

Kissing Gage would be a bad move.

Allowing any feelings beyond friendship to grow between them would be a mistake of epic proportions. An epically thrilling and totally insane mistake that would result in someone getting hurt. Namely females with the last name Kincaid.

Nope, she'd keep her hormones in check, and Gage strictly in the friend-zone from here on out. If their history wasn't enough to smack some sense into her, the way he'd burned rubber out of her driveway was.

Darcy rested her head back against the swing and closed her eyes. Stupid or not, she hadn't been able to get him out of her head. Even now, a day later, she could still smell him—leather, hot summer nights, and enough testosterone to cause flutters.

Everywhere.

"You are in so much trouble," she said to herself.

"You're in flannel pajamas with bed bugs on the pants, how much trouble can you get in?" an extremely sexy voice said, moments before she felt the cushion dip.

She opened her eyes and had to stop herself from drooling. Gage sat next to her, his arm casually strewn over the back of the swing, his legs stretched out and crossed at the ankles. His jeans hung low on his hips, his eyes sleep-filled, and his hat hiding what she could only imagine was a great case of bedhead.

He looked tired, tempting, and a little bit troubled.

"You're up early," Darcy said, knowing that Gage was one of those people who treasured his time off.

"My roommate keeps odd hours." He looked down at Fancy, who was curled up on the swing, his head on Gage's thigh. "Doesn't understand that not everyone likes to greet the sun with a morning sprint for the best tree."

Darcy found herself smiling. "And you ran out of trees downtown so you came to my hill to scout some out?"

Gage leaned his head back and closed his eyes. "Figured no one would find us here."

"Sounds like you need a cup of coffee."

He rolled his head to the side and, with one eye cracked open, took in her breakfast drink of choice and the mountain of whipped cream. By the time he got to her TEAM I DO tank top, a small smile spread across his face.

"Add a shot of scotch in there, hold the whip and the coffee, and we're good."

"Out of bed and asking for shots before eight? You must have really ticked some woman off," she said, feeling oddly weird about Gage waking up with a woman in his bed.

His smile died. "We need to talk."

Oh God, he *was* with a woman. Which meant, while she though he was about to kiss her, he had a woman. Lying in wait.

Maybe all of those sparks and compliments yesterday were nothing more than Gage just being nice, sweet, kind Gage. And she'd made something out of nothing.

Just like she had back in college.

Darcy was terrible at reading signals. Like when Kyle said she was the most beautiful woman in the world, that didn't mean he was giving up his quest. And just because Gage said she looked beautiful and perfect, that didn't mean she was perfect for him.

Which was great, just great, because she'd already decided that there was nowhere for the spark to go. Not that there had been sparks—on his side anyway.

"I agree, yesterday was fun. Kylie had fun. Fancy there seemed to have fun. It was—"

"Fun."

"Yes." She plastered a smile to her face. "Fun."

He studied her for a moment, probably trying to figure what she'd spiked her coffee with. "And did you have   fun?"

She should have lied, played it off as a casual day with an old friend. But she couldn't. Yesterday, had been a day she'd never forget. A day that Kylie would remember for always. And that was because of the kind of man Gage was. He deserved to know how special he'd made them both feel, even if it meant embarrassing herself.

"Kylie talked nonstop about her uncle last night. How you played dress up, twirled her until she got dizzy, and taught her to tie her shoes. By dinner, every single one of my shoes were laced up and double knotted. Even the drapes ended up becoming bunny ears at one point." She swallowed. "And when you showed up here, I was still riding the high of a great day, of sharing it with someone else who cares about her, and I let myself give in to the romance of it."

"The romance of it?"

"Watching you with her, remembering how close we used to be, finding that same security that always came with being around you." She shrugged. "I gave in to it."

"So, you're blaming it all on nostalgia?"

"Yes." God, why hadn't she spiked her mocha?

"You mean instead of strategizing how to make my first move back in college, all I had to do was give you my class ring and play *The Summer of '69?*"

Darcy looked up, totally and completely stunned. "You wanted to kiss me back in college?"

Gage moved in close enough that he was invading her space, filling the air until every time she breathed and all she could smell, all she could taste, was him. "I've been dreaming about kissing you since that first day in calculus when you were in that blue top and black pencil skirt."

"And pink panties?"

"Nah, it was before I got to discover all of Victoria's secrets."

They had been her power panties, bought to make her feel sexy and feminine. The rest of the outfit had set her back a whole paycheck, but Darcy had finally managed to escape her childhood, and she wanted to start her new life off right. Make an impression. And Gage had not only noticed. He'd wanted to kiss her.

"But you were dating Cheryl," she said.

"Then we broke up, but by that time you had me so far into the friend zone I knew it would take a while to dig myself out. So when Kyle wanted to take you out, I agreed. I didn't think it would turn into anything serious. You were still dealing with your mom's death, and Kyle, well he'd never done serious in his life. But then—"

His eyes drifted to her lips, and her body tingled as if he were already kissing her.

"It got serious?" she added.

"Yeah, so I backed off, because he seemed to make you happy. And more than anything, I wanted you to be happy." He cupped her cheek "But you weren't happy, were you?"

And suddenly those tingles turned to lead in her belly. "You talked to your mom?"

His expression didn't change, but his eyes hardened, enough to know that Margo had finally spoken, and Gage needed answers.

"Never mind, it doesn't matter." Needing to breathe, she stood and walked to the end of the porch.

The sun was up and cars were beginning to clog the streets of downtown. It was no longer still and quiet on her hill. The world was moving around her, and she was exactly where she'd been five years ago. Carrying a huge secret with only an Easton to confide in.

Gage came up next to her and rested his elbows on the porch rail. She waited in silence—heavy suffocating silence, for him to ask the question she'd knew he'd come here to ask. To hear the story that would force him to rethink the past, question his future, and contemplate the truth.

Darcy prepared herself for the disappointment, because at this point the truth didn't matter. He would ask her side of the story, then compare it to what he believed Kyle's to be, so he could come up with his own truth. It was what Margo had done, Kyle's mistress had done, and for Gage to do it would break her heart.

"It does matter because I should have known," Gage said softly. "I should have known something was up. You'd never walk out on someone. Ever. Not without a damn good reason."

Her heart caught. "How do you know I'm not lying?"

"Because I know you," he said, tilting her face toward his with his finger. And the absolute conviction in his expression forced her throat to close. "I know that Kyle must have really fucked up to lose your loyalty, because you are the most loyal person I have ever met. You're wary about who you trust, but once you hand over your trust, you go all in."

"We just weren't the right fit."

Gage let his head fall. "No, you had every reason to walk, and every reason to let him take the fall, but you didn't. Even now you aren't willing to sell him out." Gage looked up, and his eyes were a mixture of anger and a regret so deep she felt it all the way to her soul. "He wasn't your fit, Darcy. Not the other way around."

No one had ever said that to her. Well, her friends after the fact, but they didn't know Kyle. When she walked away from that wedding, she walked away from everyone in her life. Because at that time her friends were Kyle's friends—and she didn't want them to choose.

Mainly because she didn't want Kylie stuck in the middle, but partly because she'd never been chosen. She thought she'd been Kyle's choice, but even that turned out to be a lie.

"I don't want this to cloud your memories of him, and I don't want Kylie ever hearing about any of this. As far as she knows, she had a dad who loved her and would have done anything to be with her." Darcy closed her eyes and let the truth of the moment hit her. "Which is why we can't give in to this thing between us."

"This *thing* between us," he palmed her hips, tugging her closer, "has nothing to do with Kyle, or my family. It is between *us*." He studied her. "Or does it have something to do with Kyle?"

The insecurity she heard in his voice had her resting her hand over his heart. "You and Kyle have never been confused in my mind." And when he didn't look wholly convinced, she said, "Ever. *This thing* has nothing to do with you sharing the same DNA. But *this thing* affects everybody in our lives, including Kylie. I don't want to confuse her, Gage. I don't want her to finally get you in her life, then lose you because we have chemistry."

I don't want to get you back and then lose you again.

Once his family caught wind that there was more here than Gage getting to know his niece, it would implode. Margo would send out the hounds—and in this town that meant five strong, sexy, alpha men with piercing blue eyes and a fierce loyalty to their family. And she didn't want Kylie to become a casualty.

"Pink, this thing is a hell of a lot more than chemistry and we both know it." Gage slid his hands around her waist and tugged her even closer. "But since I know how important it is for you to sample before you decide…"

He didn't finish his sentence, didn't need to. Gage lowered his head slowly, giving her time to pull back. But she didn't, and it was the best stupid decision she'd ever made. Because the moment his lips touched hers, seven hundred volts of sexual energy combined with seven years of missed opportunity pumped through her body.

The punch so potent she felt her heart actually give a breathless *Oh my.*

"Holy Christ," he whispered against her lips. "I knew it would be amazing, but this."

She looked up into his eyes. "You can't decide after only one tasting."

"This is my kind of tasting." Gage hauled her up against him, deepening the connection.

Darcy had to agree, this was the best tasting she'd ever had. Kissing Gage was like eating wedding cake with a layer of every one of her favorite flavors—and extra frosting. It was even better. For a girl who was adamant about sampling all of the options before settling on just one, with Gage all it took was a single taste and she knew. This wasn't a case of simple chemistry.

Kissing Gage felt like coming home.

꧁

The transformation was breathtaking.

Belle Mont was not just a historic house in the hills above downtown, it looked like a festival of lights. Antique urns, overflowing with cream and white flowers, lined the brick patio and led to three long tables, which stretched beneath the canopy of giant crepe myrtles. Crystal chandeliers hung from the sky, it seemed, and hundreds of glass-housed candles were strung overhead, casting a soft golden glow over the party.

The vows had been given, the cake had been cut, and love permeated the air as couples slowly swayed to the live music, holding on to the song as if they never wanted it to end. But what had Gage's heart thumping was the sexy orchestrator standing on the other side of the dancefloor.

Clipboard in hand, her finger on her earpiece, Darcy oozed control and competence.

Dressed in a classy little black number that started at her collarbone and fell right below the curve of her knees, she stood out like a diamond in a sea of gems. Her hair was in a soft twist at the back of her neck, her eyes glimmered with excitement, and her heels hinted at the passion that lie beneath the polish.

The woman was sexy, sophisticated, and damn gorgeous.

But what had him taking a seat on her front porch, content to enjoy the view for a while, was that zipper. A single zipper that started between her shoulder blades and went the entire length of the dress.

A zipper Gage wanted to remove. With his teeth.

He could have called her the moment he got off the phone with Rhett, even saved himself the drive and emailed her. But what was the fun of delivering this kind of news when he couldn't see her reaction? Couldn't watch that sweet smile of hers take flight? He'd been a part of so many bad memories in her life, he wanted to be with her when she created an amazing one.

Darcy put up a brave front for the world, using competence as a way to fight off the loneliness and worry about the future. And that slayed him. Because Gage knew all too well how empty big moments could feel when there was no one to share them with.

He'd finished up at the office, left Fancy with a sitter, and drove straight here to help her celebrate. More importantly, he came to make sure *she* was celebrated. So when he saw that the wedding was still in full swing, he quietly made his way to the darkened cottage and got comfortable, content to wait all night if needed.

And that was how Gage found himself, two hours later, sitting in the rocking chair, waiting as the last of the employees headed home. And that was how he watched Darcy move to the center of the dancefloor and silently look up at Belle Mont House, as if to remind herself that it was all real.

And it was all hers.

Gage slowly made his way across the bridge, making sure his footsteps announced his presence.

She didn't move, not even to look back when she said, "It was a beautiful night, don't you think?" and he realized she'd been aware of him all along.

He walked up behind her so he could see the same view as Darcy. But the closer he got, he couldn't take his eyes off of that zipper, or the way her hair highlighted the bare curve of her neck.

"Stunning."

They hadn't spoken about the kiss, which abruptly ended when Kylie came bounding out on the porch, asking if he was going to stay for breakfast—which he did. Then Kylie had a playdate, so they all left the house at the same time, eliminating any chance to talk about where they stood.

Gage wasn't sure of what Darcy's reaction would be to him showing up like this. So he momentarily hesitated when she leaned back against him and said, "The Goldsteins have been married for fifty years. Fifty years and still so in love that they wanted to do it all over again. She wore the same veil as the first time and they're going back to Niagara Falls for a second honeymoon. Even staying in the same room at the lodge. Isn't that romantic?"

His answer was to silently slide his arms around her, holding her as he'd dreamed of for so long. But for all of his dreaming, and there'd been a lot, none of it had come close to holding the real thing.

"How long were you waiting?" she asked.

"Long enough to make sure your dance card was open."

"It's almost midnight, which means my dance card will expire in a few minutes."

"I guess I got here at just the right time," he murmured against her ear, then slowly turned her in his arms. "A dress like this demands at least one spin around the dancefloor."

She looked up at him through her thick lashes. "There's no music."

"Pink, we don't need music." He slid one hand around her back, settling it low on the curve, his body hardening when he felt the outline of her panties—a thong if he was guessing. "We can just sway all night for all I care."

He took her hand with his free one and pulled her close, and their bodies brushed as they moved together. Not fast. In fact, they barely moved at all, their feet taking the tiniest of steps, as the night settled around them.

"Where's Kylie?" he asked.

"Having a sleepover at Jillian's. Sam had football practice and Kylie likes to cheer him on, so after she just stayed the night."

"I think I need to meet this Sam if he's doing sleepovers with my niece."

Darcy laughed, but Gage was serious. If any kid was going to be spending time with his niece, he needed to be told of the rules. And with Kylie and those big baby blues, Gage had the feeling there would be lots of rules—and lots of boys.

Boys that were just like his brothers. Not the image he needed.

"Where's Fancy?" she asked.

"Having a sleepover at Josh's. Fancy likes to pee on shoes, so with Josh having the most expensive shoes in the family, I told him he could sit the guy for the night."

This time when Darcy laughed, it sounded like rain trickling down on leaves. Magical and melodious.

"One of the guests at the wedding wants to bring her daughter by next week," she said. "She just got engaged and is wanting a Christmas wedding. Her mother was beyond impressed with Belle Mont House."

"I think it's what you did with the house for the Goldsteins that she was impressed with." He looked into her eyes. "You are the real deal, Darcy."

"I hope so. I sent some preliminary ideas to Stephanie yesterday afternoon," she said, misunderstanding his compliment. "Just to make sure I was on the same page as what was in her head."

"She loved it." Gage slowed them down even more. "And I was talking about you. I watched you with the Goldsteins and their family. You cared about each and every one of them, making sure everything went perfectly. You have a big heart, Darcy Kincaid."

"They are entrusting me with one of the most important days of their lives, so I want to honor that." Their hips brushed, their eyes locked, and Darcy gave a look that went right down his spine to lodge in the center of his chest. "Life moves so fast, people rarely slow down to enjoy it, but love makes people stop and really see what they have. When they come here, I don't want anything else to penetrate the moment, so I create an ambiance that pulls them in, so when they think back to this snapshot in their journey together it will be as beautiful as their connection."

Gage knew enough about Darcy's childhood to know that beautiful moments were few and far between. The ones that she did have, she'd created for herself. In fact, every good thing that Darcy had, she'd fought tooth and nail for. So, he hoped when she looked back at this snapshot, it would be one about partnership and a shared joy.

"I know for a fact Stephanie loved it," he said.

"She called you?"

He shook his head. "She's still out of town. But she forwarded them to Lana at the magazine."

"Lana saw them?" she squeaked. "They were just rough ideas."

Darcy tried to stop moving, but Gage didn't want to let go, so he kept them swaying. "Rough or not, Lana loved them too."

"Loved," Darcy asked. "She actually used that word?"

Gage tried to play it cool. "Well, I didn't talk to her myself, but according to Rhett, she was impressed enough by the direction that they want to give Belle Mont House the cover."

This time he couldn't stop her from abandoning their dance. Not that he minded, since she threw her arms around his neck and plastered herself to him like plastic wrap.

"The cover? The house, not a bride in a dress, but the house?"

"Well, I think they want Rhett and Stephanie in front of the house, and probably Littleshit in wedding attire, but yeah, the house will be the backdrop."

She pulled back, and the way her eyes lit up was worth the drive, and the two hours. Hell, it was worth pushing though the past few years. "Do you know what this means?"

"That Rhett gets to be on the cover of a national magazine, his bride on one side and a glorified bunny in pink leashed to the other?" He grinned. "Owen and I are going to get the image blown up and hang it at Stout. Right above the bar."

"That means that Belle Mont House will be the number one romantic destination in the country." She was bouncing up and down now, which did amazing things for that neckline. "The August issue always puts their top pick on the cover. Oh my God," she breathed. "Belle Mont is *Wedding Magazine's* top pick for the year." She looked up at him. "I don't know how to thank you."

"Thank me? Pink, this was all you. Sure, part of Lana's original interest was because of the high-profile wedding. But the cover, that was all you."

And he couldn't be prouder.

"Not just for the help with the magazine and this wedding, but for being you," she said. "For being the kind of man to drive all the way out here in the middle of the night to tell me something you could have done over the phone."

"It's only twenty minutes." He leaned down and brushed her lips with his. "And I wanted to see your smile."

"It wasn't just twenty minutes. You wanted a kiss," she teased, but he could hear the emotion in her voice.

"That too." He gave her another one.

"But to me, it means that I had someone to share this with." Darcy looked down to collect herself, and when she met his gaze again, her heart was there. Raw and unfiltered. "Being a single mom is one of the most amazing things I have ever done, but sometimes it gets overwhelming riding out the highs and lows on my own. I wouldn't trade in a second of it, but there are times I question if I'm making the right decisions. I didn't have the best role model when it came to being a responsible parent, so it's a struggle for me to be in it alone, wondering how my choices will affect Kylie's happiness. Her wellbeing."

"You, Darcy Kincaid, are an amazing mom. You've done an incredible job with Kylie, and with this wedding. Which is why," he took her hand, "I snagged some champagne from the bar earlier. It's on your porch and probably warm by now, but I thought we could have a little toast. To celebrate."

She looked back at the main house, then bit her lower lip in a move that was all seduction. "When I saw you sitting on the porch, I asked the bartender to leave one chilling in the kitchen. Just in case."

He tugged her against him. "Just in case?"

She nodded, looking up at him through her lashes. "There's cake too. Just in case you were ready to cash in that raincheck."

"Cake always tastes better when shared."

Chapter Ten

"Second thoughts?"

Gage looked up at Darcy with her hair tumbling down her back, her bare legs dangling from the counter, and shrugged. "I might need one more taste. To be sure."

Only instead of forking off a piece of cake, he opened his mouth and waited. Darcy rolled her eyes, but offered him a bite. Meeting her gaze, he waited for the fork to slide in and felt his mouth sigh at the explosion of creamy textures and exotic flavors.

It paired perfectly with the champagne—and the company.

"That's the vanilla bean cake with mango mousse frosting. It's the one Jillian and I picked for Stephanie and Rhett. Stephanie wanted a mango martini for their signature cocktail, so I think they will really like it."

"They will love it."

"What do you think?" she asked, smiling up at him, and man, she was gorgeous. Heart in her eyes, a little bit of frosting on her lower lip, so unbelievably gorgeous it was hard not to stare.

"I think—" he said stepping between her legs and resting his palms on the counter "—that I need another taste."

"What are you doing?" she asked when he didn't reach for the fork, but instead slid a hand around the nape of her neck.

"Picking my favorite." He gently nipped her lower lip, drinking down the sweetness of the frosting, and taking his time to savor the hint of champagne that still lingered. "But, Pink, I think I'm going to need a few more tastes."

"Because you're not sure it's your favorite yet?"

"Oh, I know what I want. I even know how I want it. I'm still deciding if I want extra frosting or not."

Darcy's arms slid around his neck, but those legs. Fuck, those mile-long legs wrapped around him, locking behind his back, and putting all of his good parts in full contact with hers. "Why don't you try it this way first, and we can add some frosting later if you want."

With a moan, Gage looked her dead in the eye. "Are you sure?"

He hoped to hell she said yes, because even though he was okay with calling it a night at the cake, if that was what she wanted, the walk to the car would be damn uncomfortable.

But Gage must have been the luckiest son of a bitch on the planet, because Darcy squeezed her legs, so impossibly tight that he could feel her heat press hard against his zipper, making his eyes roll to the back of his head, and everything else go rock solid. "So sure I can already feel it building."

Gage had come here to celebrate Darcy, and since he wasn't about to miss out on a single fucking second of her night, he lowered his head and took her mouth without warning.

That kiss packed more punch than a nuclear power plant. It was one of those long-and-languid, gotta make it count, I've-got-all-night-baby kind of kisses that a man gave a woman when he wanted to make it clear just how much tasting was about to go on.

This wasn't a casual tasting, or even a see-how-it-feels-tomorrow one. Oh, no, this was a tasting that was going to last with her straight through next year. And, if he played his cards right, it would last until she forgot about his family, and their past, and couldn't imagine making any more memories without him.

Because tonight wasn't about closure, or atoning for the past. Tonight was about their time, finally taking hold of what was in front of them, and making it go the distance.

Only she moaned—into his mouth. This sweet mewling sound that was as needy as it was sexy, and Gage admitted right then, with Darcy's heels biting into his ass, that if he didn't get them to a flat surface soon, the table was as far as he'd make it.

As if reading his mind, she locked herself around his body and mumbled, "Bridal suite. Down the hall. Last door."

Gage didn't waste any time, hands on her incredible ass, mouth never leaving hers, he carried her across the kitchen. Darcy, determined to do her part, slid one of those hands, so soft and skilled, between them, giving him a massage that had him stumbling.

When he heard his zipper lower, and felt her warm skin slide beneath the waistband, his focus went hazy because all of the blood had rushed south.

Afraid they'd both wind up on the ground, he rested her on the kitchen table. "We aren't going to make it if you keep that up."

"I like keeping it up," she said leaning back. "And I always liked the look of you at my kitchen table." She pushed out a chair with the toe of her stiletto, then pushed him back into the seat. "Just like that."

"And every time I sat at your kitchen table, just like this, while you were flirting around in your nonexistent sleeping shorts, I always imagined you straddling me."

She reached out and loosened his tie. Taking both ends, she slowly tugged on it, pulling him upright in the chair. "I was not flirting around. I was cooking breakfast."

"Ah huh, like you're just helping me out of my tie."

She gave a hard tug. "Oh no, right now, I'm flirting around."

"Well, nothing says you've got your flirt on quite like straddling." He patted his lap. "And if you wanted to make it crystal clear, it might help if you lost the dress first."

Darcy turned around and coyly glanced over her shoulder.

Signal received, he ran his finger tip down her spine, stopping to watch her skin chill from the contact. When he reached the zipper, he gave one fluid tug, the teeth separated, and the dress parted in two, falling all the way to the floor—like he fucking knew it would—leaving Darcy in black panties.

No bra.

And Gage was a ninja master when it came to panties, because that scrap of black lace was nothing more than a freaking thong—and Gage's life was complete.

"Jesus, had I known that was all you had on under there, I wouldn't have waited for two hours."

"Good things come to those who wait." Darcy turned to face him, and even though she was having fun playing sex goddess, he could see the nerves in her eyes. Tell she was putting on that brave front for him.

He didn't want her courage, he wanted to make her life easier. Brighter.

"They do." This moment was all the proof he needed. "If you're not ready, that's okay."

"It's been a while," she admitted, wrapping her arms around herself like a shield. "And I'm a little nervous."

"Me too."

Standing, he cupped her face, then kissed her nose, her cheeks, and finally her forehead. And when she'd relaxed, he pulled her into his arms.

"You deserve this moment to be as beautiful as you," he whispered. "And that requires more than a table and words. I want to take you to a bed, where I can love your body, show you how special you are, and then in the morning wake up to your smile and start all over." He tilted her face to meet his. "And if that isn't tonight, then it isn't tonight."

Her eyes shimmered, emotion and desire turning them the warmest shade of whiskey.

"I'm done waiting, Gage. I'm ready to move forward. With you." Silently she took his hand and together they walked down the hallway, to the last door, and once they were inside, Gage scooped her up and carried her to the bed.

Setting her down, he tossed a condom on the nightstand, his tie over the back of the footboard, and his shirt to the floor. His eyes never leaving hers, he slid over her body and gently kissed her lips.

"What about your pants?" she asked.

"This is all about you. We're going to take it slow, wait until you are good and ready."

A man of his word, Gage took his time, licking and kissing and memorizing every part of her body. Starting with her breasts, high and a perfect handful, before moving south, loving how her breath caught when he nipped her breast, licked her stomach, and finally kissed a whisper above her core.

His lips were careful to get close enough to tell her what was coming, but not giving in to the fire until he'd made his way down each one of

those legs he loved, kissing her on the inside of her ankle as he slipped off
her heels. He spent extra time working his way back up to her inner thigs,
nipping the patch of bare skin right beside the lace edging of her panties.
And when she was panting so hard he knew she was ready, he gave a lick
right up the center.

"Oh…God," she cried out, arching her back to increase the friction.

And since he loved the sound of her crying out, he did it again. On
the third pass, he upped the ante, tugging her thong to the side and leaving
nothing between them but hot, pulsing skin.

"I'm about ready to—"

She broke off as he gave a little bite, only to soothe it with his mouth.
"We've had too many almosts, Pink. This time, I'm going for the sure
thing."

Even though she was about ready to combust, he worked her until her
thighs tightened, closing in around him, straining for more. Gage, always
the gentleman, gave her what she wanted, adding a finger to the mix.

Only when she made this sweet panting, almost gasping for breath,
did he push her over the edge. Her climax was hard and sudden, and she
pushed off the bed, her entire body coiling as Gage kept going. Relentless,
he kept on, right through her release, and through her aftershocks, not giving in until she was limp on the bed, a satisfied smile on her face.

"That was amazing."

"Better than cake?" he asked.

"Way better than cake," she murmured, her eyes sliding closed.

While she caught her breath, Gage made short order of his pants and
was back over her in a matter of seconds, sheathed and ready to go. But he
paused, right at her core.

"What are you waiting for?" she asked, opening her eyes.

When he still didn't move, her eyes opened and locked on his. Two
big, beautiful pools of sunshine that were for him—and him alone—he let
himself fall.

With the hope that she would catch him.

"That," he said. "That was what I was waiting for."

Unable to hold back any longer, he gave one long thrust and filled her
completely, both of them gasping at the connection. Energy arched and

flowed between them, and he realized he had a dopey smile on his face. Which wasn't as embarrassing as he'd expected, because Darcy's expression wasn't that far off.

"I knew it would be great," she said.

"But this is—"

"Yeah."

Thanking God that he wasn't alone in this insanity, Gage began to move. Slow withdrawals and even slower thrusts, building a rhythm together until it was as if they were back out on the dancefloor, moving to the sound of their hearts.

Darcy shifted her hips, ever so slowly, locking her legs around his back—those heels once again biting into his ass.

"Your shoes are killing me," he moaned.

"Want me to take them off?"

"Fuck no."

With a throaty laugh, she squeezed her legs even tighter, until there wasn't any air left between them—and he was certain he'd have puncture wounds come tomorrow. And when the languid pace became too painful to sustain, Gage braced himself on an elbow, so he could stroke every inch of her, find every spot that made her gasp.

When he found *the* spot, she didn't just gasp, she gripped his hair and crushed her mouth to his. And damn, she could kiss. The mouth of an angel, the passion of a tornado.

Addicting combination.

"Now," she said, biting his lower lip. "I wanted to be clear. I'm ready now."

Perfect timing, since he was one stroke from losing it, and the little swivel action she did with her hips didn't help his situation. Breathing became impossible. Holding back became impossible. His chest felt too big for his skin and his heart too full for his body.

He wanted to hold her to him and set her free all at the same time. So when she lifted her hips, he went in fast and deep. Sure, he wanted to make this last, wanted to blow away every "what-if" she'd had about them, but she was clenching again, thrusting those magnificent breasts out. And the pressure built. Hotter and higher.

He tried to keep himself in check, but her thighs tightened around his waist until he thought he'd pass out.

"Pink," he said, the nickname only he'd ever used, and she opened her eyes and met his gaze straight on. She was looking at him as though he was her choice—and that was all it took.

She started to shake and she pushed down as he came up and then, *holy fuck,* then the sweetest sound ever came out of her mouth.

"Gage," she cried. Not once, but several times. Each one gaining in volume and ferocity.

"I got you." *But do you have me?*

He must have said it aloud, because she whispered, "I've always had you."

With one final thrust, he pressed his face into the curve of her neck and let go. Loud and hard, his release shook him to the core, as if tearing him in two while putting him back together.

He rolled over, bringing Darcy with him as they both struggled to catch their breath.

When he was able to open his eyes, Darcy was resting on his chest, her smile tilted up at him.

"Hey there," he said, picking up a strand of her hair and letting it slide through his fingers.

"You know what's even better than day old cake?" She kissed his chest. "After-sex cake."

"You know what follows after-sex cake?" He fisted his hand in her hair. "Eating the frosting. One. Lick. At. A. Time."

Chapter Eleven

"It's so sinful, I could lick every last drop."

Stephanie Stone set her shot glass down and placed a dramatic hand to her flat stomach. She was dressed in a cropped pantsuit, strappy Jimmy Choos, and a handbag that cost more than Darcy's mortgage. She was regal, refined, and so stunning Darcy had a hard time not staring.

Today was a perfect Portland afternoon for a tour and menu tasting. The roses were in full bloom, the sky was so clear they could see all the way to Mount Hood, and a cool breeze came off the Columbia River. Yet, Darcy was a nervous wreck.

Today wasn't just any tasting, it was the Easton/Stone wedding menu tasting.

Outside of Gage, Rhett would be the first Easton she would reunite with. While things with Gage were going well, so incredibly well she couldn't stop smiling whenever she thought about their night together—which was every day this week—she wasn't sure how welcoming Rhett would be.

Gage assured her that everything would work out. That Rhett was beyond grateful for her willingness to work with them on the wedding, the rest of his brothers were coming around, and he'd handled his mother. But when Stephanie showed up with her publicist instead of her betrothed—a strange arrangement as far as Darcy was concerned—she began to wonder if Gage had been too optimistic.

If the chasm between her and Kyle's family was too painful to overcome. And, if so, where would that leave Darcy and Kylie?

Gage was a man of his word, and she was secure in his promise that she wouldn't get burned. But he was intensely loyal to his family. And in the end, Kylie might be family—but Darcy was an outsider.

Always would be.

"Rhett was all for the shooters," Stephanie said, looking at the different types of shot glasses, picking up an elongated modern style.

"I think when you said shooters, he was imagining something a little more leaded than chilled artichoke and avocado soup," her publicist Anna said. Taking a tentative sniff, she wrinkled her nose and put it back. "Plus, it's green. Rhett specifically said nothing green."

Darcy had to laugh, because Kyle also had an acute aversion to anything green. Actually, if it was labeled a vegetable, he'd claim he'd get hives just from looking at it. Kylie had the same reaction.

But since this wedding was a joining of two people, it was Darcy's job to make sure both sides were represented.

Even if the groom was a no show.

"You could always go with this softened watermelon and mint sorbet if you like the idea of a chilled shooter." Darcy placed a glass in front of each woman, since it was clear from Stephanie's book that she wanted some variation of an elegant shooter passed around on trays. "Or, we could have the chef make up a refreshing shaved ice, such as key lime to freshen the mouth and cool the guests as they wait for dinner to begin."

Stephanie took a dainty sip of the watermelon sorbet and her eyes went wide. "It's light, refreshing, and delectable." She downed the rest in a single swallow. "It's like watermelon sangria."

"There's actually a little rum in there. I knew that you loved fruit inspired drinks, so we modeled this after a mojito," Darcy explained. "There isn't enough alcohol to be overpowering, and we'd of course have virgin ones for guests who don't drink, but it's different and would go well with the rest of the meal."

"Anna, you should try this." She slid the shooter Anna's way, and her assistant took an obligatory sip, and gave a smile. Then she picked up her phone and started scrolling through emails.

The woman wasn't there as a support for Stephanie. She was there because she was being paid. A bride should be surrounded by family, friends, and if not the fiancée, then at least someone who wanted to celebrate the moment.

Stephanie acted as if nothing was amiss, but the poise and posturing was a defensive tactic Darcy knew well.

"Didn't I see a cantaloupe one on the list?" Stephanie picked up the menu book and flipped to the second page. She pointed to a cantaloupe and ginger sorbet. "Can we try that one? The color would look great against the bright orange poppies."

And this was why it was important that both people be present.

The last thing Darcy wanted to do was overstep her bounds, and make the situation any more uncomfortable. But avoiding a possible allergic reaction was more important.

With a bright smile, Darcy said, "It would look amazing, great eye. Anna, could you go ask the chef if he could whip one up?"

If either woman was surprised that Darcy was asking Anna to do her job, neither of them showed it. When Anna disappeared into the house, Darcy gently asked, "I didn't want to ask in front of Anna, but isn't Rhett allergic to cantaloupe?"

Stephanie blanched. "He is? I didn't know." She gave an embarrassed smile and, not for the first time that day, looked as if she were trying to pass some test, rather than planning her own wedding. And wasn't that a sad state of affairs. "That's something I should know, right? I mean we're getting married. In three weeks and I nearly ordered something that could send the groom to the hospital."

Darcy put a hand on Stephanie's arm. "If you wanted to reschedule when Rhett is back in town, I'd understand." It would create a bigger time crunch on her end, but she was willing to work something out, if anything to save Stephanie from a disastrous wedding menu. "I know you two are both on crazy schedules, and the wedding is in just a few weeks, but I want to make sure both of you love the day."

Stephanie shrugged. "He was called in last minute to be on the Tonight Show, which is huge for him. He offered to cancel, but I told him to go. Opportunities like that can change a career, especially when he is so close to that tipping point. He gets back tomorrow night and I leave Wednesday morning for LA. I know this probably sounds like a mistake, but we really are good together."

"I've seen a lot of weddings, and it isn't about knowing someone's favorite color or sports team that matters, it knowing what's in their heart." Something that Darcy had learned after Kyle. She'd known everything there was to know about Kyle, except what really made him tick.

"I thought that dating someone in the industry would be easier, because they'd understand the demands." Stephanie sat back and she looked tired, more than just the stress of a wedding. No, her kind of tired came from feeling responsible for everyone around her. "But we're both constantly feeding the demands, and sometimes it feels as if we're being pulled in opposite directions. We're rushing the wedding because it's the only time we both have two weeks free for over a year."

Darcy was never for rushing a marriage unless it was for love. And not just from her own experience, but from a decade in the industry. Yet, she was the last person to be giving marriage advice. But she was an expert in knowing when to run for the hills. "When you're together, does it feel right?"

Toward the end, even when she and Kyle had been in the same room, Darcy felt like he was a million miles away. She'd known for months that it wasn't going to work—it had just taken her heart longer to catch up. Darcy didn't give up on people, she'd been given up on too many times to do that to anyone else. So acknowledging that her relationship was over was difficult.

Going through with the wedding would have been suffocating though.

"When I'm with Rhett, I feel like I can kick back and be myself. He's sweet and caring. So easy to be around." A light sparked in Stephanie's eyes. "The man treats me like I'm something special, not for anything I've done, but just for being me, you know?"

"Yes." Darcy did know. It was the same way she'd felt with Gage. Back in college and the past few weeks. He had a way of making her feel seen, as if who she was was enough.

Until Darcy had become a mom, she'd never been enough for anyone in her life. Even the people who were supposed to love her unconditionally had found her coming up short. With Gage, she felt as if she exceeded his expectations.

"We might have only known each other for less than a year, but it feels right," She let out a big breath. "With the media taking bets on how long we'll last, and Margo putting so much pressure on this wedding being perfect, sometimes I think it would have been easier to elope."

Darcy wanted to tell her to fly to Fiji, marry her man, and stay as far away from Margo as possible. Then again, she still hadn't heard Stephanie say a single word about love. It was clear that she loved how Rhett made her feel, but she hoped there was more.

But this wasn't her friend, it was her client. And she'd hired a planner not a therapist, so Darcy said, "This day is about you and Rhett. And I know how mothers-in-law can be." She also knew firsthand how Margo could be. "I will do everything I can to make sure the day remains about celebrating you and Rhett."

"Oh God." Stephanie covered her mouth, a look of embarrassed horror taking over her delicate features. "Here I am going on and on, and I forgot that you went through all of this. I don't know the whole story, but Rhett told me enough that I should be thanking you for even letting us get married here, not complaining about Margo."

"Rhett was always wonderful, so I'm happy he wants to get married here." If she left out how he'd never contacted her after the wedding, it was the truth. "And you shouldn't have to miss out on the venue you want because of a situation you had no control over."

"Which is why this wedding has to be perfect," Stephanie said, and she sounded so close to tears, Darcy slid her another watermelon shooter. "I want to look back and have it be about us. Not about if one of the warming trays went out, or if the food didn't reach expectations."

"Yours and Rhett's expectations are all that should matter, and if we stick with that, it will be all that you imagined."

"Although I am hopeful, the follow through is yet to be seen."

Darcy didn't have to look up to see who had crashed their tasting. The censure and oversweet scent of Margo's perfume was enough to have Darcy cringing—and Stephanie turning pale.

Bracing herself to look into the woman's eyes who made her life a hell, Darcy turned around. And the first thing she noticed was how frail Margo looked. She's always been a petite woman, but the sorrow she'd worn like a coat all those years had taken its toll. Instead of feeling angry, Darcy just felt sorry for the woman who had buried two men she loved.

"Margo," she said, standing and offering her a seat. Margo was dressed in a flowered skirt and blouse, perfect for tea—or the mother of the groom. And if Stephanie didn't ask her to leave, Darcy wasn't going to. She might own Belle Mont, but this wasn't her wedding. So it wasn't her place. "I didn't realize you were coming today."

"And miss my daughter-in-law's tasting?" Margo gave Stephanie a kiss on the cheek, then took her seat. She didn't kiss Darcy. Didn't even look her way. "As soon as I heard Rhett was in New York, I drove right on over. No bride should have to do a tasting alone."

"Thank you, Margo," Stephanie said, sending Darcy an apologetic look.

Darcy winked at Stephanie, to put her at ease, then picked up the empty glasses. "You're right on time, Margo, we were just about to go over the options for hors d'oeuvres. If you ladies will give me a moment, I can see where the chef is at with the plating."

"Actually, I need to use the powder room. Can you show me where it is?" Margo asked, and Darcy momentarily froze. She didn't know how much the woman knew about Kylie, or how she felt about the information, only that Gage had told her she had a granddaughter.

"I can take you," Stephanie offered, her eyes going between the two women.

Darcy nearly wept with relief.

The last thing she wanted was to be alone with that woman. Nothing good could come from it. Then again, Gage had said she'd softened, and he had hope. Darcy would have to take heart in that. If there was any chance for forgiveness and a fresh start, then, for Kylie's sake, Darcy would even take the first step.

"That's okay, Stephanie, I've got it." Darcy put an arm out to usher Margo. "You finish up that last watermelon shooter and I'll take Margo to the ladies' room, then check on the hors d'oeuvres."

"Thank you." Margo stood.

Neither of them said a word as Darcy led her into the house, nor when they were in the empty hallway, so when they reached the bottom floor restroom, Darcy pushed her pride and feelings aside and said, "About Kylie—"

"Gage told me how much you have taken under consideration, and how generous you are being with our family," Margo interrupted, and the weight that Darcy had been choking on slowly started to lighten. "He said that you have been more than accommodating for Rhett and Stephanie."

Darcy blinked. "Rhett and Stephanie?"

"Yes, that is what we are here to talk about today, is it not?"

Unsure of what Margo wanted her to say, or even why she was there, Darcy decided to follow her lead. Gage had promised to handle his mother, promised that she'd changed, and maybe this was her way of proving to Darcy that she was willing to work in the confines of what was best for Kylie.

"I want them to have their dream wedding," Darcy said. "And that means having their family be a part of it. I understand that."

"Do you?" she asked, and suddenly Darcy didn't feel so light anymore. "Then why would you shut us out of Kylie's life all these years? You and I planned your entire wedding, and not one word about the pregnancy. That is not how family behaves."

The sorrow in Margo's face was heart shattering. Darcy didn't know how she'd feel if she were in the older woman's shoes. Losing Kylie would be like losing a part of herself, finding out that a piece of Kylie was still out there—and Darcy never knew?

A deep ache formed, just thinking about it.

The difference was, Darcy would have never lashed out at someone the way Margo had lashed out at her. And instead of regret in the older woman's eyes, which should have been beneath some of that sorrow, there was residual anger.

And that had Darcy worried.

"You weren't my family, Margo. You made that clear the night I came to you for advice," she said, feeling every helpless emotion she'd felt that night. "As for knowing about Kylie, that was Kyle's call to tell you or not. He chose to keep you in the dark, not me."

Margo stepped back, her face pale as if the words had broken something loose deep inside, and she was torn between disbelief and heartache. Darcy could go into the dozen or so reasons Kyle had for not telling his mom. But since none of them would help in the healing process, and all of them were cruel, she remained silent.

Margo believing her didn't change the truth. And hurting the woman wouldn't change the past.

"But after the funeral," Margo said, skating over Kyle's actions. "And every day since, that was your decision. You had no right to deny me of her!"

The emotional force of her words had Margo holding onto the wall for balance. Her face was drawn and her hands shaking, but her eyes were hard. Resolved.

"I am her mother, and a damn good one, so I have every right," Darcy said. "And I am only open to introducing her to you *if* we can find some common ground and move past whatever this is between us. Which Gage believes we can."

"Gage has always been overly optimistic."

"I believe there is hope," Darcy said quietly, because, surprisingly enough, even though she'd had her share of run ins with the force that was Margo Easton, she did have hope.

Gage believed they could come through this. Darcy believed in Gage's strength. Most importantly, she believed in his character.

"It was never my intention to hurt you or come between your family. I just wanted to love Kyle, and then do what was right for Kylie."

"Your kind of love nearly destroyed this family once, and I won't let it happen again." Margo was a few inches shorter than Darcy, but still managed to look down her nose at her. "Gage assured me that *that* won't happen, but Gage has always had a soft spot for this damsel in distress act you do so well. I am no fool. I know he's been spending time over here."

Darcy's face flooded with heat. She felt as if she were a girl again, being told she wasn't good enough. But she wasn't a girl, she was a twenty-eight-year-old woman, and Kylie's mother. Regardless of what Margo thought, or what happened with Gage, Darcy knew what *her* family deserved—and she wasn't willing to settle.

"Gage is getting to know Kylie. And we are getting to know each other again, outside of the past and his family."

"My family is finally healing, moving on from the tragedy that struck, so you need to leave him alone."

Darcy wanted to point out that they weren't all hit by lightning. Kyle's impulsive nature had caused the breakup, the accident, the devastation.

And holding onto the anger wasn't going to change that. But she thought of Gage.

And finally Kylie.

Fueling this hostility between them wouldn't help anyone.

"All I want to do is move on too. We both deserve to find happiness again." And knowing that with people like Margo, one had to take a stand and fight for their footing, she got up close and personal. "But right now this is about Rhett and Stephanie's happiness. So while I won't stand for you tossing around blame in my house, I won't ban you from the wedding. Now, if you choose to be a part of Kylie's life, that depends on how *you* choose to conduct yourself."

Gage had received three calls from Rhett over the past few hours. All of which he'd sent to voice mail. First, because he'd been in a series of meetings. And second, he was not about to be suckered back into dog sitting. He'd finally achieved a solid night's sleep and was determined to go for the gold and get two.

So when he got a text saying, *Call me, Asshole,* he sent one back. It was a photo of him waving hi to Rhett—with his middle finger. But when Stephanie called, Gage knew something was up.

It took her the exact length from his office to his mom's house to explain Margo had crashed the wedding tasting and, although Darcy hadn't asked her to leave, there was a weird vibe.

And by weird vibe, he knew that his mom had somehow overstepped her bounds. So by the time he pulled into his childhood home, his imagination had come up with enough possibilities that he felt sick.

Leaving the flowers he'd picked up on the way out of work for his girls, he'd taken to thinking about them that way, he walked in and dropped his coat by the door. "Mom, you home?"

He didn't have to go far to find her. Margo Easton, the strongest woman he knew, was sitting in the living room in her favorite reading chair. She was wearing her slippers, a Sunday dress, and her floral house robe. The same one she'd worn since he was a kid. Her hair was tucked back in a bun, she had a full face of makeup on, and she was clutching a photo album.

"Mom," he said again.

Margo looked up and Gage's temper vanished. It was hard to be pissed when your mom looked as if she'd been crying.

"I didn't hear you come in." With a shaky smile, she patted the arm of the chair. "Come and sit. I was just going through these old photo albums. Look at this one of your dad and me."

Silently, she traced a shaky finger over a photograph, worn around the edges and faded. Gage sat on the edge of the chair and—*holy hell*—his lungs stopped working.

It was a shot of his parents doing a dramatic dip under the neon light that still hung above the front door at Stout. His dad was dressed to impress in a collared shirt and a skinny tie, and Margo. Wow, his mom looked like a woman in love.

She was warm and alive, her eyes lit with so much joy it was hard to reconcile that with the woman who sat next to him. He'd forgotten just how all-encompassing their love had been. They were a team, in everything they did, refusing to even spend a night apart in the twenty-nine years they'd been married.

One time, when they'd gone to visit his dad's grave, like they did every Sunday morning, she'd admitted to him that the years without her Benjie felt like a long goodbye that had no end. It was no secret that Margo had fallen into a deep depression after his death, but until this moment, Gage hadn't realized that she never fully recovered.

"When was that taken?"

"The night he opened his bar." Margo clutched his hand, and when she spoke, her voice was so fragile it made swallowing difficult. "He'd worked so hard for that bar, scrimping to get the down payment. Grandpa Easton offered to give him a loan, but Benjie wouldn't hear of it. He was determined to make it on his own. He was a man of his own making." A nostalgic smile teased her lips. "He's kind of like you in that way."

"What did Grandpa say?"

Clark Easton made his fortune in the lumber industry back in the thirties, leaving behind a legacy for his family. All of his sons had followed in his footsteps, except one—Benjie. Benjie loved brewing and he loved beer, but most of all he loved talking to people.

But being an Easton, he didn't open any ordinary brewery. Oh no, Benjamin Easton turned his dream into a money press, blending his two loves, and creating one of Portland's premier brews. By the time Gage and Kyle came along, Stout had five different locations around the state, and sold their brand nationwide.

"A black sheep can always get more for their wool."

Gage noticed an elegant box sitting on the end table. Its lock was broken, and the leather strap cracked, but the outside was in impeccable condition. "What's that?"

"My love box." She picked it up. "Did you know that your father wrote me a love letter every week when he was away at Stanford? Every week for six years, he never missed a one. Said his love grew so much every day that he'd explode if he didn't tell me."

"That's Dad," Gage said, thinking back to all of the times Benjie would pull him aside to tell him he loved him—just because. Benjie believed that love needed to be let out so it created more room to grow.

"He was a wordsmith, that's for sure. It's where Rhett gets his love of writing songs," she said, slowly flipping through the envelopes, not really seeing any of them. "When Benjie came home from college he still wrote to me every week. Can you imagine?"

Yeah. Gage could. His dad was one of the greatest men he knew, and his capacity to love was astounding. His love got this family through a lot, and there were times Gage wondered how much better they all would have fared if he'd been there to help them through Kyle's death.

"Getting the bar up and running, raising six kids, even through cancer," she said, her voice sounding far away. "He'd sign them, Eternally Yours, no name. Just Eternally Yours, then put a stamp on them and mail them, even though we lived in the same house." She put a hand to her mouth and shook her head. "Isn't that ridiculous?"

"No, that's commitment."

His mother looked up, her eyes soft and lost. So damn lost Gage hunched down on the balls of his feet and took her hands. "What's going on, Mom?"

"After he passed, I still got notes. For about a year. He'd written them ahead, knowing he wasn't going to beat the cancer." She pulled a letter out of the back of the box. It had been read and reread so many times it was as thin as tissue paper. "This was his last one, he told me in it that it was his last one. He'd written it while watching me beside him in the hospital. I didn't leave the house for a week when I got it. I couldn't. Walking outside, looking at everyone living their lives, knowing that mine had ended was too much."

"Oh, Mom."

"But then that Friday, the postman came, and I went out to check, to see if maybe he'd been wrong and was able to write one more." She smiled. "And there was one."

"He wrote another one?"

"No." She took a moment to swallow the emotion. "It was from Kyle. A little love note for me, telling me how much Dad loved me. And every week, on Friday just like your dad, a note from Kyle would arrive. I don't know if Benjie asked him to, or if he did it on his own. But those notes made your dad seem not so far away. But then Kyle—"

She broke off and held the letter to her chest. And Gage had a hard time holding everything in his chest together. Because she'd lost her son and her husband in the same accident.

"Kyle died and the letters stopped," he guessed.

She looked at the album one last time, then her eyes filled with tears. "No. He proposed to Darcy, then the letters stopped."

Ah shit. "Please don't put that on Darcy," Gage begged, because he knew, in his gut, that she wasn't the problem. A year or so before his accident, Kyle had begun to grow distant. Skipping bar night, missing family dinners, and it was Darcy who encouraged him to make time for his family. "That's on Kyle. He started spending more time away from everyone, even me."

Mother fucker.

Gage knew exactly why Kyle had started acting weird around family—because he'd been up to no good. Even as a kid, whenever Kyle got a wild hair up his ass, he'd start acting weird. Keeping secrets, spending time away from home, coming home late and smelling like trouble. It was as if he didn't want to disappoint his family, but wasn't willing to toe the line.

So he'd kept the two worlds separate.

"I blew it," she whispered. "I couldn't take not being able to see her, see what my granddaughter looked like, and I ruined everything. I thought if we met, the girl would want to come visit, and I blew it."

He pulled her into his arms, suddenly aware of how fragile she felt. How small she'd become. "Whatever happened, I can fix this."

"She won't let me see Kylie now, I know it," she said into his chest. "She took Kyle away from me, and then Kyle's daughter." She looked up and wiped angrily at her tears. "What kind of woman keeps a grandchild away from her grandmother?"

"A mother who wants to protect her daughter from pain and disappointment," Gage said softly. "Darcy's a great mom, and she's doing the best she can."

When Margo didn't look convinced, he said, "Look at it from her perspective. She's overwhelmed being a single parent, struggling to ensure Kylie's wellbeing. She has to work twice as hard to give Kylie a safe home. Now, throw in five Eastons and a mother-in-law once removed who had her arrested for breaking and entering." Gage chuckled lightly. "Can you blame her for being cautious?"

"*I* was being cautious when I called the police," she defended. "I thought she was going to clear out Kyle's things without letting me go through them. What might be trash to someone else could be a treasure to a mother. And it wasn't her home, it was Kyle's."

"They had lived together there for over a year."

His mom called the cops because she blamed Darcy for Kyle's death. Plain and simple. It was easier than blaming her son who was gone. But Gage didn't even want to go there. Not tonight.

"The easier we make things on Darcy, the quicker you'll get to meet Kylie. So no more sneaking around. We wait for an invitation."

"What if the invitation never comes?"

"It will come," he said. "You just have to be patient."

Margo shook her head with defeat. "I was patient before, waited for Kyle to realize he was rushing into marriage, but time ran out and I lost my son. I won't lose the chance to know my granddaughter."

"You won't lose Kylie," he promised. "But pushing for the sake of pushing, isn't going to move things any faster."

"I'll trust you then, because patience isn't my strong suit."

That's what Gage was worried about.

Exhausted and covered in yellow and green frosting, Darcy plopped down at her kitchen counter. It wasn't even dinnertime, and she was already dreaming about bedtime. Or a sugar-rush. She'd gobbled down two cupcakes from the reject pile—with extra frosting.

It hadn't helped.

After the disastrous confrontation with Margo, Darcy had barely managed to pull it together for the rest of Stephanie's tasting, then another couple who wanted to tour the house for an eightieth birthday party.

"I need a vacation."

"You need to get laid," Jillian said, and Darcy sent her a glare. "I know the look of a woman who needs to get laid. I see her every morning when I brush my teeth. And you need to get some man action."

Jillian was piping rose leaves on a line of mini-cupcakes for the opening of a lingerie shop in town. Crumbs clung to the ends of her hair, and black food dye stained her fingers.

"I did that, and then his mom showed up," Darcy said, although the idea of a little more alone time with Gage sounded like the perfect way to make up for a crappy day. She remembered how creative he'd gotten with after-sex cake, how they'd both been covered in frosting by the time the sun rose. Then she remembered the knowing look in Margo's eyes and shivered. "I have no idea how such a spiteful woman could have raised such great boys."

"One good parent can outweigh a bad one. Trust me," Jillian said. "Speaking of boys, did you tell Gage what happened?"

"I wasn't sure if I should call or not." Darcy stood and, reaching for the red edible glitter, sprinkled a thin layer over the piped roses. "I know he had meetings all day, so what would I say? 'Hey, sorry to bother you in the middle of the million dollar deal you're negotiating, but your mom came to my house and hurt my feelings'?"

"You aren't bothering him. You both agreed to the terms and his mom chose to ignore them. So maybe you could call and say, "Hey, your mom stopped by today and words were exchanged. I wanted to see you so we can talk about how to handle this as a team." Jillian set the piping bag on the counter. "That's what people do when they think they might want to be in a relationship that extends beyond knowing the other's O-face. Or so I've heard."

Jillian's soon-to-be-ex wasn't the best when it came to teamwork. He was more of a scream out orders from the sidelines kind of teammate. One of the many reasons they were no longer together. Plus, like Kyle, he suffered from a slippery dick.

"You're right, it's just this whole *trust me* thing that Gage has going on is not something I've had a lot of positive experience with."

Trusting someone to know how to get you to make on O-face was one thing. Trusting someone to stand by your side when the opponent was family was a whole other ball game.

"Giving someone the opportunity to disappoint you, doesn't mean they will," Jillian said. "You can live safe, or you can live happy."

"What if I want both?"

"Buy a vibrator. But be warned, they aren't much to cuddle with on cold days." Jillian leaned in and winked "Especially if you've been cuddling with arms like that."

"What?" Darcy asked, just as Kylie came racing down the hallway. "Uncle Gage is here! Look, Sammy, that's my Uncle Gage."

Darcy turned and saw Gage standing on the other side of the screen door. Their gazes met and she felt herself tingle. He stood there in his leather jacket, looking big, bad, and oh so edible.

His dark hair was tousled, as though he'd driven with the windows down and the top back. Dressed in a pair of slacks, a white button up that was unbuttoned to work's-over, and a smile that said *I know what you look like underneath that dress*, he left no doubt that he'd been thinking about their night too.

The part that had her going all mushy was the summer flowers in his hand. Not one bouquet, but two. One made entirely of violets. The other comprised of every pink summer flower she could think of.

"Hey, Tiny," he said when Kylie opened the door for him. He squatted down low, and offered her the small bouquet. "These are for you."

Kylie took the violets and baby's breath and breathed them in, making a big deal to close her eyes. "Are they for my birthday?"

He glanced at the cookies on the counter, the frosting on Darcy's hands, and his mouth made the perfect circle of *Oh shit.* "It's her birthday?"

"No, her birthday is November seventh." Darcy wiped her hands on a towel and walked into the entry. "I think she was wondering what the occasion was."

"Yeah, what's the occasion, Uncle Gage?" Kylie repeated.

"There doesn't need to be an occasion to bring a beautiful lady some beautiful flowers," he said, his eyes on Sammy. "Right, son?"

"Ah huh," Sam said, but his face said he thought flowers were wussy.

"You must be Sam." He extended his free hand to take the boy's smaller one, shaking it. "Nice to meet you."

"You're really big," Sammy said in complete awe of Gage. Compared to his own father, who was a weasely accountant, Gage must look like a superhero.

Darcy had to admit, right then she thought he looked pretty heroic too.

"You should see the rest of my brothers. They're bigger than I am," Gage said. "We came super-sized so we could look out for our niece."

Sammy looked at Kylie and tilted his head. "She looks out just fine. Doesn't even run into trees when she's twirling."

"Good to know." He ruffled Sammy's hair, then looked at Darcy. "These are for you."

"Oh my," Jillian whispered from behind. "Maybe I've been on my feet too long today, but I think I just swooned a little."

Yup, Gage Easton was a class act—and worthy of her trust. She just hoped he was worthy of her heart, because in one move he'd completely stolen it. He was backing up his words with actions. Something completely foreign, and thrilling, for Darcy.

"I'm Gage, nice to meet you," he said, shaking Jillian's hand.

"I'm leaving." Jillian wiggled a brow Darcy's way. "I was just telling Darcy how I was going to take the kids out for ice cream. Kids, grab your coats."

"They haven't even had dinner," Darcy argued, but the kids heard ice cream and were already piling out the door chanting. "Ice cream. Ice cream."

"Seriously, you don't have to take them out." Darcy knew her friend had hours of work still left for tomorrow's delivery. She'd come over to use the professional kitchen and have Darcy help with the decorating so she could make her deadline.

"Oh, yes I do." Jillian leaned in and whispered, "If not for you, then for all of the single ladies who will never get the chance to show a man like that their O-face."

Gage smiled.

"It was nice to meet you." Jillian grabbed her purse and didn't stop until she was at the front door. "Oh, and don't rush, I'm taking the kids to the park afterward. We'll be gone for at least an hour. Maybe longer." She walked out, hollering over her shoulder, "In fact, I'll text before we head home."

And the screen door slammed on its hinges.

Gage's shoes echoed off the wood floor, not letting up until he was standing close enough to touch. Close enough to smell. His gaze tracked her from her eyes to her toes, eating up her tousled hair and floured apron, giving a sound of male appreciation when he got to her bare feet.

"From the looks of all that frosting in there, Pink, we're gonna need a hell of a lot more than an hour."

Chapter Twelve

*D*arcy's body liquefied as she remembered how he'd eaten his way through an entire tub of frosting the other night.

"So you came for another tasting?" she asked, playing with one of the flower buds. It was a stargazer, her favorite.

He watched her fingers dance along the bouquet, and let out a frustrated groan. "No, I came here to see if you were all right. I heard my mom paid you a visit."

She looked at the flowers and sadness swelled as the magic slowly faded. "Oh, so these are an *I'm sorry my mom's crazy, please forgive me,* bribe?"

"No. These I got before I talked to my mom." He took one of the flowers and ran it along her cheekbone, the silkiness of the petals erotic against her skin. "These are *You are so fucking beautiful I can't get you off my mind* flowers."

"Oh," she whispered.

"Yeah, oh." He scooted closer, their bodies brushing. "So, you want to talk about today?"

"Not really." There was already a conversation in progress that she was more interested in continuing. "But Jillian thinks we should talk about today, and she's usually right about those kind of things."

"Ah, and what did Jillian say?"

"That I should open up to you. Tell you the problem so we can figure out a solution together."

"Jillian is a smart woman." Gage set the flowers on the counter and took her hand. Leading her to the family room, he pushed aside a pile of Kylie's dress up clothes, and took a seat.

"It's kind of annoying." Darcy started to sit next to Gage. "She has this way of cutting to the, whoa, what are you doing?"

Moments before her bottom hit the sofa, Gage tugged her sideways and into his lap.

"I don't want there to be distance when we talk. The whole way here, all I could think about was this gap that could have formed and I didn't like how it made me feel." He leaned back and pulled her against his chest. "I like how this feels though."

"Me too," she whispered, and pulled her feet up so she could curl up in his lap.

"I'm sorry about my mom," Gage began. "I know there is no excuse for what she said, or for barging in on you after she promised to wait until Kylie was ready. But she is just sad and lonely and scared. She thinks if she can control everything, then she won't experience loss, when all she's doing is pushing everyone away."

Wasn't that what Jillian had just accused her of doing? She was too scared to open up and really trust someone, for fear of being let down. But if she never lowered her walls and let someone in, she was denying herself the joy of finding companionship.

Love.

Darcy tilted her chin up toward Gage, choosing her words carefully. "I can understand where she is coming from. She's lost a lot in her lifetime. And I thought about just calling the whole thing off."

Gage stopped breathing. She could actually feel his lungs cling to the oxygen, refusing to let go.

"But then I thought of you." She touched his cheek. "How much laughter and joy you've brought into my life in just a few short weeks, and how if I had been too scared Kylie would have missed out on all of that too. How I would have missed out on this. I would have missed out on you, Gage, and I can't even imagine what that would have been like."

At her words, Gage released the breath. The stress lines bracketing his mouth softened and that terrified expression vanished. And a beautiful warmth spread through her entire body.

"I don't trust your mom, but I trust you," she said, realizing that it was the truth. She'd trusted Gage from the moment they'd met.

Although it had felt as if he'd broken that trust when Kyle died, now she knew that he hadn't. He hadn't abandoned her out of anger, or even turned his back on her. He'd done what he'd thought was best—for the both of them.

And now it was time to for her to be honest.

"What I'm saying is that I trust in what we have. More than my fear of being hurt or the need to cling to control. More than the little voice in my head that reminds me everyone I have ever trusted has let me down." And looking into those deep blue eyes, she let go—of all of it. The history, the baggage, the fear. Leaving room for whatever magical road this relationship might take. "I am willing to trust what I love most to you, Gage. And that's my heart and my daughter."

The air vibrated between them, rich and real, and neither one of them shied away. They stayed in the moment, so much being said, yet no words were exchanged. But the longer they stared, the calmer Darcy felt, and the more she realized that this—*this* was what she'd been looking her entire life for.

He was who she had been waiting for. Which was ridiculous since he'd been in front of her the whole time. She'd just been too scared to admit it.

"I've got you," he said, his voice so rough it was nearly a growl. "I know how hard your trust is to come by, and what a beautiful gift it is, so I promise you that I will never betray that gift again. Ever. My father was a man of his word, and I want to be that kind of man. For you and for Kylie."

Ever so slowly he took her lips, gently—no, lovingly—kissing her. It wasn't sexual or leading, it was a promise. A beautiful vow he was making to her. She could feel his honesty, sense his devotion, and taste his love.

Love.

There it was. Darcy was in love with Gage and it wasn't scary or uncomfortable, evoking that desperation she'd always associated with the emotion. With Gage, love felt safe and warm, like the wonderful bonds that she'd read about, but, outside of Kylie, had never experienced.

The love she'd had with Kyle had been born from a young woman looking for a family and happiness. What she felt for Gage came from a woman who was already happy, looking for someone to share that happiness with.

"Make love to me," she whispered against his lips. "I want to feel this—" she touched her heart "—everywhere. And I want to feel it with you."

He took her hand and rested it over his chest. She felt the strumming of his heart, pounding just like hers. "I have felt like this since the first day I met you. It grows stronger every day, even when we were apart it never seemed to stop. I couldn't get you out of my heart, no matter how hard I tried."

"Then stop trying."

Darcy captured his mouth.

This kiss wasn't slow and languid, it was driven by hunger and desire, and something else. Need. Her body pulsed with need—for him.

Darcy needed him as much as she needed her next breath, and she'd prided herself on never needing anyone.

Love didn't leave room for pride, she realized, as he deepened the kiss, taking her to another world—to his world.

His hands stroked her back while he spread kisses across her cheek to her ear, "What color do you have on today?"

Darcy gave him a wicked grin. "You'll have to find out."

"Come here," he ordered, helping her straddle his lap.

With a groan, his eyes dropped to the buttons on the front of her sundress. There were a lot of buttons. In fact, they ran the entire length of the garment. Gage didn't seem to be concerned, taking his time to undo each one, his eyes darkening further with each pop.

When he reached the one at her waist, he hesitated for the briefest second, then parted the material. With a grin that was as boyish as it was sexy, he said, "I guess it's my lucky day, Pink."

"I've found a new liking for the color." She shimmied her shoulders and the dress pooled around her waist. But when she reached for her bra strap, he caught her hand and placed it against his chest.

"Give me a second. I've been dreaming about this day for a long time, and it was too dark the other night to pay these the respect they deserve."

Gage reached out and gently weighed them, one then the other, finally pushing them together so her breasts fell over the top of the pink lace. "Damn, you are perfect."

He leaned in, taking them in his mouth and Darcy let loose a needy sigh. His mouth was lethal, licking and nipping all the right places, worshiping her until she was panting.

"I think I've been dreaming about this for just as long," she admitted, threading her hands in his hair and holding him to her.

Her confession urged him on and his hands slid under the skirt of her dress, greedily moving up until he found the string of her panties.

"Also pink?" the words vibrated against her nipple and her breath caught.

"Also pink." She slid against his hardness, frustrated at all of the material between them. "And in the way."

With a smile that was hot enough to melt the sun, Gage hooked a finger around the band and yanked. They came off with a tear and Darcy's hands went to his belt, working to get the buckle undone.

Gage brought her face to his, and this time the kiss went from hot to nuclear meltdown in no time flat. Darcy had his jacket off, his pants undone and was freeing him when he flipped them around. Darcy was flat on her back, her dress around her waist like a hula-hoop, and looking up at the most amazing man she'd ever met.

And it couldn't have been more perfect.

"Come here," she repeated his earlier order, and tugged him down.

Cupping her jaw, he obliged. His mouth was firm, just like the rest of him, and when his hands slid down and with purpose, she parted her legs. His hands were almost as earth shattering as his mouth, remembering what she liked, delivering just the right amount of pressure to drive her insane.

He stroked and loved, bringing her to her breaking point in record-breaking time. It was almost embarrassing how easily he could read her, how intuitively he played her body. And even when she was about to explode, he pulled back and reached for a condom.

"One more stroke," she begged.

"Pink, I'm going to stroke you until you're screaming my name. And when you come, it's going to be with me inside of you, and we're going to do it together," he said, and then slid home.

And home had never felt so good.

"Together," she said.

Gage put a hand beneath her head, the other splayed on her butt, and his arms tightened. When they were so close air couldn't even slide between them, only then, did he begin to move.

Darcy's body matched his rhythm as if they'd done this a thousand times in the past. And maybe they had, in dreams. Gage didn't kiss her, didn't speak, just locked on her gaze and never looked away.

The connection was immediate and intense, and every nerve ending in her body reached out for him. Every seed of hope she'd buried over the years came back to life and wrapped around them. Took them higher until there wasn't anything there except them—and the amazing, wonderful, and infinite possibilities.

They were moving in harmony, completely in sync and together. Gage was stroking a fire in her belly and forever in her heart. Every thrust brought them closer. To what, she wasn't sure, but it felt all encompassing. And she wanted to get there.

With him.

"Gage," she said, feeling the tears form, but not understanding why she was crying.

"I got you," he said. "Just let go and I'll be right there with you. I promise."

Darcy's body tightened, coiling harder and harder, and when she couldn't hold on a second longer, she burst from the delicious pressure. Hard and fast—and Gage was right there like he promised, taking her as high as she could fly, and cradling her when she came tumbling back down.

Darcy clung to him, her face pressed into his neck, her arms so tight around him they were shaking. Her whole body was shaking. She was relieved to realize, so was his.

Gage was holding her as if promising to never let go. Which was okay with her, because there was no other place she'd rather be than in his arms.

And in his heart.

Chapter Thirteen

he sun was still high when Gage arrived at the Belle Mont House, with a tool belt around his waist and a cold six pack of Stout hand-crafted cream soda—as per request.

Tomorrow was the 100th annual Heirloom Bloomers Tea, and he'd offered to help set up all the custom made easels. In exchange, Darcy had offered to make him dinner. Since tonight was his family dinner at the Eastons, she suggested they move Finger Food Friday to Saturday Sandwich Sit-down.

He'd been looking forward to it all week. The chance to spend time with his girls, around the kitchen table, was what he'd been hoping for all along. That Darcy had been sweet enough to move her schedule around so he wouldn't be in a position where he had to choose, spoke volumes about her heart.

"Tell me it's cold," Darcy asked, wiping the sweat off her forehead with the back of her hand.

She stood in the middle of the rose garden in a pair of white snug shorts, a big straw hat, and gardening gloves. Her top was where things got interesting. It was tight and a light yellow that—*look at that*—turned translucent in the sun. Which meant that he could see clear through to the bra she wore beneath. Also a light yellow. And lace. Designed to cover right above the nipples and drive men bat shit crazy.

Darcy had been fighting with a weed when he drove up, and apparently the weed had won. Because she was sweaty, dirty, and sexy as hell.

"Right out of the fridge at the bar." He held up the six-pack and dangled it like bait.

He was baiting her all right. A gentleman would have walked it over, but then a gentleman wouldn't get to watch those hips swish back and forth as they made their way across the brick walkway.

"My hero," she said with a secret smile just for him. "I've been dreaming about this for hours."

His eyes raked over her. "Want to know what I've been dreaming about?"

She grabbed a bottle and twisted off the lid. "Incoming."

Gage turned, just as Kylie came racing across the field. Dressed in a pair of overalls, a doggy shirt, and one of Darcy's hats, she looked like a mini-Heirloom Bloomer.

"Uncle Gage," she hollered, flinging herself in his arms.

He'd barely had time to set down the cream soda and catch her. "Hey, Tiny. I missed you."

"Me too!" She wrapped him up in a hug that knocked her hat right off, and knocked all of the stress right out of his week. "Did Mommy tell you?" She looked at Darcy. "Did you tell him about the fishing trip?"

Darcy grinned. "I was going to let you do that."

"Fishing trip?" Gage hadn't been fishing since—well, since his dad died. It was one of the things they did, just the two of them.

Each brother had their own special Dad and Son outing. It was Benjie's way of giving each one of his kids focused attention. Josh and Dad used to go hiking. Rhett's time had been spent playing guitar, Owen's brewing beer, Clay's was Seahawks games, Kyle's watching NASCAR. And Gage's had been fishing.

Just him and his dad and the stillness of the day.

"I love fishing."

"You do?" Kylie asked, her face so expressive Gage had to give her another hug.

"I do."

"He likes it, Mommy," she yelled, as if Darcy were across the lawn and not right next to them. "Then, you can be my partner?"

"Anytime."

Anytime, anywhere, and for anything.

There wasn't much either one of the Kincaid ladies could ask him that he wouldn't do. They both had him wrapped around their fingers. And they were securely wrapped around his heart.

"He's my partner!" Kylie wiggled out of his arms and the second her feet hit the grass she started jumping up and down. "You don't have to dress like a boy now."

Gage lifted a brow in question and Darcy laughed. "It's the Daddy Daughter Fishing Day at the river downtown. I threatened to dress like a boy to fit in with all of the other dads. But when Kylie asked me if you could take her, I said she needed to ask you."

"You're not my daddy, but you're a boy and an uncle. So I figured that counted, and this way Mommy doesn't have to pretend to like fishing."

She shrugged. "It's the worms that get me."

Gage opened his mouth to say he'd bait every hook if that meant he got to take Kylie on her fishing trip, but nothing came out. Everything he wanted to say, to Kylie and her amazing mom, was stuck behind the lump that had lodged itself in his throat.

He never imagined that a little thing that could fit in his pocket could capture his heart so thoroughly. And it wasn't because she was Kyle's. Sure, in the beginning that was what had started his determination to be a part of her life.

But after getting to know her, watching her spin in circles on the grass, experiencing one of her hugs, Gage had fallen. Fallen hard for this tiny thing. He'd fallen for her mom too.

"I'm in," was all he could manage, and when he looked up at Darcy, she was looking back, tears sparkling in her eyes. She was all in too, she'd told him as much the other night when she'd asked him to make love on her couch.

That's exactly what it had been. Making love and making promises to each other. Promises he wanted to spend a lifetime keeping. He didn't just want to sit around that dinner table tomorrow, he wanted to sit around it every night, and then again every morning.

He wanted to spend his Sundays watching his girls play in the garden, while he wrote them love letters. But his love wasn't singular like his mom's. His love was big and full, and strong enough for the both of them—and whoever else came along.

Gage's heart stopped as the realization washed over him. This was real and honest and he felt giddy with joy.

"Ms. Kincaid," a voice said from behind and Darcy took off her hat. "Yes?"

Gage turned around to see a man in a suit and tie, with slick shoes and a slick attitude, and an envelope that had the power to destroy everything. But before he could intercept, the man asked, "Darcy Leigh Kincaid?"

"Yes," she said again, getting ready to sign for a package like this was some check from a client or a shipment of wedding cards.

But there were no cards. Gage had received packages like this before, and had even sent a few over the years. He'd never meant for one to be delivered to Darcy.

"You've been served," Slick said as soon as Darcy's fingers closed around the envelope.

Her face went from curious to uncertainty. But Gage was certain of exactly what was in there. And who it was from.

"Served?" Darcy opened the envelope. "I don't understand. By who?"

"I'm just a messenger. Have a good night." Then Slick disappeared as if he hadn't just handed them all a sentence.

Hands shaking, Darcy stared at the letter, unable to make out the words. She could see each symbol, even knew what they were, but she couldn't put them together to form the actual words. Maybe it was her heart that wouldn't let her because it was slowly breaking.

"Mommy, what's wrong?" Kylie asked, wrapping her little arms around Darcy's leg and resting her head against her hip like she used to. She hadn't done that since the first day of preschool last year, and Darcy had thought she'd outgrown leg hugs.

But there she was, doing it again, and all Darcy could do was stare at the summons to appear at a hearing. A hearing to discuss custody of Kylie. Her Kylie, who she had raised from birth and never gone a full day without seeing.

Without hugging.

"Don't worry about this," Gage said, not sounding surprised.

Why wasn't he surprised? And why did he look so calm?

It had felt like a one-two-punch to Darcy, the blast so unexpected she wanted to sit down. Right there in the grass. But Kylie was giving her a leg hug, and she didn't want it to stop.

"Darcy, I will handle this, I promise," he said, the determination in his voice so fierce she wanted to believe him. But the words she was finally starting to understand said that she couldn't.

"Why is your mom suing me?" she said, her voice stronger than she felt.

"I don't know." He took the paper and read it over. "She's suing for custody of Kylie?"

"Mommy," Kylie said, her voice thin, and close to tears. "Sammy said his dad got custody and he has to do sleepovers on some weekends. I don't want to stay with his daddy on weekends."

Darcy got down on her knees and took Kylie in her arms. "You're not going anywhere, honey. I promise you. Now go in the house and see if we have any cupcakes left over for dinner."

"I don't want cupcakes." Her little breath was coming in short bursts. "I want to stay with you."

"I'll be right behind you, I just have to go tell that man he delivered the letter to the wrong house."

"You'll give it back?" she sniffed.

"I'll give it back," Darcy said with a smile, even though it was so tight she was afraid it would crack. But Kylie wasn't upset about the letter, she didn't even understand the letter, she was upset because Darcy was upset. *Time to pull it together.* "Now, go on and get those cupcakes ready and maybe we can watch 101 Dalmatians while we eat them."

"Kay," she said and walked toward the cottage.

Darcy watched as her daughter trudged up the front steps and into the house, waiting until the door shut, all the while Darcy's heart was breaking.

"I swear to God, Darcy, I had no idea."

She spun around, this time not trying to mask her anger. The fear, she hid that, only to be pulled out later tonight when Kylie was asleep and Darcy was alone.

"Then why does it say," she snatched the summons back, "*Mother is overwhelmed and admitted to struggling to take care of child's wellbeing?*" She looked back at Gage, everything inside of her willing him to come up with some answer to explain away the hurt. An answer that would make everything okay, and bring them back to how it had been only minutes ago.

But he didn't explain it away, didn't tell her it was a misunderstanding. He ran a hand down his face, that beautiful face Darcy had trusted with her kid's life.

"She twisted my words. I was telling her what a great mom you were, reassuring her that she'd get to meet Kylie and…" he faded off. "I am so fucking sorry."

"Sorry doesn't cut it." She slammed the papers against his chest. "Sorry doesn't take back these words that are printed, that Kylie could someday find and wonder if they were true. Wonder if she'd somehow done something to overwhelm her mom to the point that she struggled to raise her. Because I know that burden, Gage. And I have worked my ass off so that Kylie would never have to carry that."

"She doesn't have a case," he said as if it made a difference. "This is just her way of, well, being Margo."

"Do you think I give a shit about this hearing?" Angry tears burned her eyes. "I care that my little girl is upset. I care that the man I trusted used my words against me. Words I said to him in an intimate setting. We were about to make love when I said those words. Or at least that's what I thought it was."

He stood there, silent, and she was certain it was because he could see the disappointment tighten around her neck, watch the pain cut right through her chest. Piercing her heart and leaving nothing unmarked.

"I can fix this," he pleaded, sounding heartbreakingly desperate. "Don't let her ruin this. Ruin us. I made a mistake."

"Sometimes things slip, accidents happen. But I was clear up front about my concerns. I thought I had made it so nothing like this could happen again." She met his gaze, her own so watery he was a blur. "So that you couldn't possibly let me down."

"Darcy." He reached out to touch her and she stepped back.

"I asked you one thing, Gage. Just one." And It had seemed so simple to her. "To put Kylie first. And you didn't." She hated the way her voice cracked. "Tell your mom if she doesn't drop the suit, she will never see Kylie." She swallowed. "I think you should go."

"Please, don't do this," he said, and she had to look away because he was starting to cry, and Gage didn't cry. Ever. Not even at Kyle's funeral.

Darcy put her hand to her heart, to keep it from shattering to the ground. "I told you before, I choose Kylie. I always will."

Chapter Fourteen

"You going to get up?" Rhett asked, towering over Gage at the gym, sipping from a water bottle. "Because Fancy wants to know when you're going to return his Biggest Pussy on Earth sash."

"Fuck you," Gage said

"Didn't you hear? I'm engaged. Plus, hormonal agents aren't my thing. They mope around all day and leave the seat up."

Gage kicked out his leg, swiping Rhett's feet out from beneath him and sending him crashing to the gym mat. Water went everywhere.

"The bigger the asshole, the harder the fall," Gage said, pushing himself up and off the mat while Rhett brushed the water off his pants. Which only managed to make him look like he wet himself.

Damn, that felt good. First time he'd smiled in days. Too bad it was short lived, because the second his lips twitched, he remembered that he had nothing to smile about. Margo wasn't dropping the lawsuit, Darcy wasn't returning his calls, and somehow Rhett still got to walk down the fucking aisle at Belle Mont House.

Not that Darcy would be there. She'd explained to Stephanie that, under the circumstances, she would be taking off a few days before the wedding. She and Kylie were flying down to Disneyland for a long girls' weekend. And, okay, that made him smile.

Tiny would love meeting the princesses and would buy an autograph book for them to sign. He could picture her twirling down Main Street in one of those costumes they sell in the shops there. She'd probably even get Darcy to wear a matching one.

And Darcy would look sexy as hell.

"You going to Friday night dinner this week?" Rhett asked. Grabbing two towels, he tossed one at Gage, who caught it midair. He used the other one to wipe the sweat off his face.

"Nope."

"You going tomorrow then?"

"Mom isn't home on Wednesdays. She has her bridge club meetings."

Rhett looked up from the towel. "I was talking about Darcy's hearing."

Darcy.

Even her name brought on an ache so deep Gage had to check his chest to make sure there wasn't a hole in it. And he knew what Rhett was talking about.

Margo, who admitted she'd just sent the papers as a warning, refused to drop the suit. Claiming that the family lawyer was certain that, although she wouldn't get custody, it was likely she would be granted some kind of visitation rights. Or at least it might scare Darcy into caving.

That was the hope.

His mom was a fool to think Darcy would cower when it came to Kylie. She would take on the Taliban if it was for someone she loved. Nope, the only thing this harebrained idea of his mother's would do was cause Darcy to sever all ties with his family.

With him.

"I called and asked if she wanted me there. She didn't return my call." She hadn't returned any of his six dozen calls. "I took that as a big no."

At this point, he doubted she'd ever talk to him again. She'd built a great life for her and Kylie, then let him in. And what had he done? Brought the reign of his entire family right into her home and tore it to shreds.

Gage and Rhett walked into the locker room. Gage opened his locker and took out his phone, checking to see if he had any messages.

"So then, that's it?" Rhett asked. "You're just going to bail?"

Gage slammed his locker. "I'm not bailing. I am respecting her wishes."

"Isn't that pussy for bailing? Because it sounds like it got hard, you fucked up, and now you're leaving her hanging to deal with the aftermath. And Mom." Rhett cocked his head, then blinked. "Sorry, man, for a minute there I thought you were Kyle."

Gage grabbed Rhett and pushed him up against the lockers, a loud bang echoing through the room. "This has nothing to do with Kyle."

Rhett looked at Gage's hands, which were fisted in his shirt, and lifted a brow. "Could have fooled me."

Gage wasn't so sure anymore either. Kyle was the hot head, the one who acted first and expected someone else to clean up his shit. And that's what Gage had done his entire life. Clean up after Kyle.

Kyle was gone and Gage was still dealing with his messes.

"Fuck." Gage let go of Rhett's shirt, but not before giving his brother a final shove.

"You tore my shirt," Rhett whined like a little girl. "It's my favorite."

"Your dog shit in my car."

"We're even on the shirt, but not the cheap shot. You've got one coming."

"Whatever." Gage sat on the bench and, resting his elbows on his knees, let his head hang. "I'm so tired of all this shit."

"It's about time." Rhett poked at the hole Gage had torn in is shirt, then sat down next to Gage. "I don't know how it all went down, and I don't know how you're going to deal with Mom, but I do know that you've waited a long time for her," Rhett said. "And I would hate for you to miss out again because you were once again too afraid to tell her the truth."

"I did tell her the truth, then I screwed it all up." Gage let his head fall against the locker. "All I ever wanted to do was protect her, and somehow I managed to hurt her all over again."

"Then, fix it," Rhett said, as if it were that simple.

Nothing about this was simple. Gage could negotiate his way out of a Thai prison if he had to, but he couldn't figure out how to give Darcy what she wanted and not bring her more grief.

"I don't know how," he admitted, hating the feeling of being helpless. "Margo will always be Margo, and I won't put Darcy through having to deal with her. And Kylie, *man* that little girl deserves the world."

"So you'd rather sit here, crying on my shoulder because you can't make a choice."

Gage froze, because wasn't that exactly what Kyle had done? He couldn't choose, so he did nothing and lost it all.

Gage didn't want to be that kind of man. And Darcy deserved more from a man than that. Gage wanted to be the kind of man who Darcy could count on.

The kind of man she could trust, who never disappointed her, and if for some reason he did, he found a way to make it right.

"Dad would choose love." He'd probably send her a letter every week for the rest of her life until she knew she was loved. That she was special.

Rhett smiled and smacked him on the back. "So you admit that you love her?"

"Hell, yeah, I do." Gage grabbed his keys and headed for the door. "I gotta go."

"Tell Mom I say hi."

To think that Darcy had considered Kyle's funeral as the worst day of her life. That was a walk in the park compared to standing outside a mediator's office, with a handful of character witnesses on call to attest to the fact that Darcy was a great mother.

Because Margo hadn't just filed for custody, she'd filed under the guise that Darcy wasn't fit to raise Kylie. Which meant that the authorities were involved now.

Talk about irony. When Darcy had needed someone to step in on her behalf, make sure she was well fed and had clean clothes to wear, there had been no one. And now, she'd given everything she had to being the best mom for Kylie, yet she had to convince a panel of strangers she wasn't struggling to give her daughter the very thing that came so naturally.

Love.

"You sure you don't want me to come in with you?" Jillian asked. She was not expected for another hour, but she'd come down to offer support.

"No, I think you have to wait until they call you in." Darcy thought about walking into that big room and fighting for her daughter. Alone.

It was a place she'd become familiar with, but now that she'd tasted how nice it was to have someone in her corner, alone suddenly felt daunting.

Margo had her lawyer and her condemnation to keep her company. And Darcy had—

"Oh, no, don't do it. Don't you let that woman get in your head," Jillian said fiercely. "You are the best mom I know, and there is no court in the world that wouldn't see that."

"That's what I'm worried about," Darcy admitted. "That Margo will get enough traction that this case actually goes to court. Can you imagine Kylie sitting in a judge's chambers and answering questions about her home life?"

"I know. I think about that every day with Sam, which is why I decided to settle out of court with Jerry." Jillian took her hand. "This won't go any further than today."

"How do you know?" she asked.

Jillian pulled Darcy into her arms. "Because you're the nicest person I know and bad things can't happen to nice people."

Darcy had an entire lifetime of experience to make a strong case against Jillian's theory, but for now she decided to believe. It was easier than the alternative.

A big mahogany door opened, and a petite woman in a suit and glasses peeked her head out. "Miss Kincaid, we are ready for you."

Darcy's stomach twisted into knots, and her heart raced. With one final squeeze, Darcy let go of her friend, and immediately felt the cold rush of what she was about to face overtake her.

Time seemed to slow with each step she took, the buzzing in her head going faint, until she was acutely aware of every sound in the building. She took in a deep breath, put her shoulders back, and channeled that same brave girl who had more first days at a new school than she did friends.

"You never have to fake it," she whispered to herself. "You've already made it."

She was a college graduate, a successful business owner, and a fantastic mom. A few of the many things she'd accomplished all on her own.

She was prepared to do this alone too.

But when she walked in the conference room, it wasn't Margo and her expensive lawyer sitting across the table.

It was Gage.

Dressed in a dark suit with his negotiating face on, he looked up at her and smiled—and she wondered if this was one battle she wouldn't have to fight alone. Or if karma was so cruel that she'd have to take on the one person she couldn't win against.

"Sorry for the wait, Pink," he said, walking over. His eyes were calm, and locked on hers. "I was just telling Mrs. Lamont about our picnic."

"Our picnic?" she heard herself ask over the pounding of her heart.

"The one we had in the park. I was telling her about playing dress up with Fancy, and how much fun Kylie had putting on a doggy fashion show."

Still unsure of why he was there, of whose side he was on, she lowered her voice. "If this is about seeing Kylie, I'm not going to cut you off, Gage. You know I wouldn't do that. She adores you and you make her happy."

"You always look out for Kylie. I know that. And these people know that too," he said. "But I'm not here for Kylie. I'm here for you." He took her hands in his bigger ones, his thumb stroking her lightly, as if giving her some of his strength. "I'm here to make sure you're looked out for, and that you're happy."

Darcy looked around the room. "Where's your mom?"

"At home, thinking long and hard about where she wants to stand in my life."

"The suit?" She looked at the mediator, her heart wanting so badly to believe, but afraid to hope.

"It has been dropped," she said, taking her things and standing. "I apologize for any inconvenience this may have caused, but when a concern is brought to our attention, it is our duty to look into matters. Thankfully, Mr. Easton clarified things."

"So, that's it?" she asked, needing to hear the words with her own ears.

"That is all from us." The woman smiled as she was exiting the room. "But I do believe, after the story I heard, that your Mr. Easton has some more groveling to do."

The door shut, leaving her with *her* Mr. Easton. "Thank you," she said, so many emotions rushing at her she felt dizzy.

"You have nothing to thank me for," he said softly. "If anyone should be saying thank you, it's me. I busted into your world and listed all kinds of demands that you had no reason to listen to. But you did, because you are a good person and a great mom. You let me get to know Kylie, and you let me get to know you, and I promised you I'd protect you. Then at the first sign of trouble, I bailed."

"I told you to leave."

"I should have stayed," he said. "I should have stayed and been there to ride the low with you. You aren't the one who is struggling, it's my family. I wrote you a note that said you deserved the man my father raised me to be. I was wrong."

Darcy tried to pull free, but he held on tighter. "You deserve the man I was born to be. I love you, Darcy, and I should have told you that the first time I realized it. You are so easy to love, and you deserve to hear those words every day."

She melted at the romance beneath his statement, but held strong. She didn't want to give in to romance again, only to wake up and find it was nothing but a fairy tale. She wanted the real thing.

"Words are easy, Gage, it's the follow through that's hard."

"You once told me you chose Kylie. You chose Kylie because it was the easy choice. You're my choice, Darcy. Loving you is the easiest thing I have ever done. Let me love you the way you deserve to be loved. Let me be the lucky son of a bitch that gets to wake up every morning loving you and go to bed loving you even more. Let me be the man I was born to be, because around you I am him. I promise, if you let me back in your heart that I will protect it with my life."

"Is there an expiration on this offer?" she asked quietly.

"Love has no timeline. And if it takes me coming back every day to tell you, then that's what I'll do," he said, the truth shining in his eyes so bright it was her undoing.

"I don't want you coming back every morning, because that means you left." She looked up into is eyes. "The only place I want you, is next to me," she said through a small sob. "I feel like I've been chasing love my whole life, and now that I've found it I never want to let go."

"I've been chasing you for nearly a decade, and now that I've finally have you in my arms, I'm never letting you go."

"I guess we make a pretty good team," she whispered.

"You know what happens next?" he asked, his eyes heating.

"We eat cake?"

"We kiss." He laughed, and Darcy felt it vibrate through her whole body as his mouth came down on hers in a kiss that really did have the power to change the world. Her world.

When her eyes slid closed, she could feel the sway of their bodies and with each step the weight of the past lifted away, making room for all of the love they were going to share in the future.

Read on for a sneak peek of Marina Adair's next
heartwarming romance from her new series
The Eastons
<u>Promise Me You</u>
Available Summer 2016

Chapter One

If this was what marital bliss felt like, then the only boyfriend Delaney Hart would ever commit to in the future would be battery operated.

It wasn't so much that some guy had spilled his beer down the front of her overpriced dress. Or even the fact that she was two shots into the night and the rehearsal dinner hadn't even started. Nope, what had Laney flipping the universe the big one was that the only man she'd ever wanted to *have and to hold* was about to marry someone else.

"Ball and chain locked and loaded," Owen Easton said from behind the bar, a big ass grin on his face. "I can't believe my kid brother's actually going to get hitched tomorrow."

Neither could Laney.

"Next there'll be a mess of kids and our band will go by way of the diaper genie." Paul, the band's bass player slurred, making it obvious that he had drowned one too many sorrows.

There wasn't enough alcohol in the world to numb Laney's pain.

Ever since Rhett Easton, local pop rock star and legendary ladies' man, announced his shocking engagement to one of the internet's biggest fashionistas, the band had been scared. Scared that his new wife would grow tired of the long stretches on the road, scared that she'd convince him to go solo—like their label had been pushing for—and scared because they all knew damn well that without their front man, guitar prodigy Rhett Easton, Subtle Warfare was going nowhere fast.

Laney was scared too. So scared she hadn't slept in weeks, her headaches coming more frequently, until she couldn't drive a car without fear of having to pull over.

Over the past few years, Rhett had gone from writing partner to friend, and eventually the man who taught her that it was okay to trust. He was the only person in the world who really got her—looked past her hang-ups and saw the woman she could become.

The only thing she was in danger of becoming, at the moment, was sick.

"Well, at least he'll have a hell of a honeymoon. I know it's wrong to covet your bro's woman, but man, oh man," Paul finished with a long look at Stephanie, who stood under the twinkle lit gazebo with Rhett, slowly swaying to the live band.

"Honeymoon? They should have saved the money and stayed home for all the sightseeing they're going to do," one of the other band members joked. "Hundred bucks says they don't see anything besides the hotel room ceiling."

"Two hundred, they never even make it to the bed," Paul jested.

This kind of crude banter was normally reserved for poker night or nights on the road after a gig, but since Laney was always seen as one of the guys, they didn't temper their discussion for her. Normally it didn't bother her.

But tonight it did. Because it symbolized the end of her dreams for love, family, children, and eternity. Rhett was it, and yet his dreams lay in the perfect poise and beauty of the woman standing next to him.

From her vantage point at the bar, Laney was able to see the bride's slim back, her delicate sheath dress trailing to the floor.

Stephanie Stone was tall and elegant, her glossy golden curls spilling over her shoulders and onto the white silk of her dress. Eyes brimming with emotion, her smile spoke of a woman about to be married. Her unwavering poise showcased her family's deep money roots. Her confident nature spoke volumes of the benefit a supportive and wonderful family offered.

Stephanie was stunning, well-educated, perfectly feminine, and everything Laney could never be.

"One more," she said, and her agent, Gage Easton, came up beside her and leveled her with a look. "What? It's a wedding celebration. Look, I'm even wearing a dress." She lifted her light orange colored dress, which Stephanie had hand-picked, and she was sure was the epitome of fashion.

"The color is cantaloupe whimsy and it has no straps, so Stephanie used some kind of sticky tape to hold it up. Tape, Gage. I deserve another shot."

Gage lifted his hand to order another round, then took the stool next to her. "Or you could learn from my mistake and tell Rhett how you feel rather than just walk out that door and disappear."

"You mean walk up to him and say, 'Hey, I got you the silver chafing dish off the registry, which will sure come in handy on the tour bus. Oh, and by the way, I know you're about to get married in front of five hundred of your closest friends and family, not to mention the press, but I think I like you. Check Yes or No'?"

Gage's eyes went soft with sympathy. "Or, how about, 'I know you think of me as a little sister, but my feelings for you have changed. I thought you should know, because pal-ing round with you hurts. A lot. And it's making our working relationship really hard on me'."

Today wasn't about her. Or the band. It was about Rhett, and she understood that this marriage was the right move for him. Stephanie was well spoken, sophisticated, and would be the perfect wife for his booming career. Also, she wasn't terrified of commitment.

"When Father Paul said, 'speak now or forever hold your peace,' by not speaking up, I non-verbally, verbally agreed to the silence forever clause. And I take non-verbal verbal agreements seriously." She sent Gage a pretty convincing smile. "You, as my agent, should know these things."

Gage rested a hand on hers, and even though her survival instincts demanded that she jerk it back, she forced herself to remain still. "What I know is that you have two choices, either say something or walk. Both will tear you up, but not telling him will haunt you forever."

"I'll be all right," she assured him. "I just need some time."

All Laney knew was tough love. As a kid she learned it was easier to say she was all right, even if she wasn't. As an adult, she'd learned to just keep smiling. But nothing about this moment was ever going to be all right.

She could tell him that she was finally ready for a relationship.

But that would be a lie. And Laney had promised never to lie to herself again. Even for love. She'd done that once, and only recently gained the strength to leave behind the binding web of lies. She was still figuring out who she was. She couldn't risk losing herself.

It might not seem like it now, but this change was for the best—for everyone involved.

"What's one more haunt to keep me company?" Laney picked up her shot and, with a salute, downed it, then stood.

She'd known what needed to happen when she'd agreed to come to the rehearsal. So, without a backward glance, she moved toward the door. In her attempt to go unnoticed, she knocked over a barstool and, unaccustomed to wearing anything higher than converse, stumbled into something strong, solid, and body-meltingly warm.

"Where are you sneaking off to, Trouble?" Rhett asked, and that low gravely timbre of his that made him a superstar, rolled right through her.

"I don't sneak," she said, refusing to meet his gaze since his BS meter was always set to high around her.

"I know sneaking when I see it," he said with a chuckle. "And you're sneaking. Out of my rehearsal dinner."

"I'm not sneaking," she said, looking at his hands. His big, masculine, almost-married hands that had grabbed her waist to keep her from falling. "And for your information, I was looking for the ladies' room."

"The ladies room is behind you. And the exit, that you were making a beeline for, would be in front of you. Just past the rose garden, the hoard of guests waiting for dinner, and your pride."

"Fine," she admitted. "I was sneaking."

"I know." He sounded *so* smug. "You always look like you want to cry when you're contemplating something illegal."

She snorted. "Leaving a dinner, in which you aren't obligated to pick up the tab, is hardly illegal."

"It is when your fiancée thinks your best friend hates her," he said quietly.

"I don't hate her," she said looking up and—*oh God,* how was she ever going to say goodbye when those eyes of his drew her in.

They were deep and bright, and the color of a gentle rolling sea. So mesmerizing she was actually standing in a dress in the middle of a wedding rehearsal, waxing poetic in whimsy.

She needed to get a grip.

"Then what's going on?" he asked. "You bailed on the last few weeks of the tour, you cut out of the bachelor weekend early, and you've been avoiding us all night."

You. I've been avoiding you.

"I'm not a playing member of the band. I help you write songs." Her throat closed, because after tonight she wouldn't even do that. "We weren't writing anything, so I came home. As for the bachelor weekend, I cut out two days early."

"It was a three-day trip?" "The guys were talking about going to a strip club. I don't do strippers."

"That's a shame." His eyes roamed down her body, slowly coming to a stop at her heels. "Because you in those shoes with a stripper would have made for one hell of a bachelor party present."

Even though she knew he was teasing her, an unwelcomed, but all too familiar heat surged through her body. When it reached her cheeks, she smacked him in the chest, averting his attention.

Unrequited love sucked—but not nearly as much as would if he learned about her unrequited love the night before his wedding.

"Ow," he said. "And I don't do strippers either." She rolled her eyes. "Okay, well just that once, but she was in grad school and liked classic rock, and we dated for almost a month." Which before Stephanie would have been considered a serious relationship for Rhett. "And I'm not that guy anymore. I'm getting married tomorrow and my best friend won't even give me one dance before she bails."

"Gage is your best friend."

"He isn't wearing a dancing dress."

Rhett's fingers slowly slid around to her lower back and pulled her further into his strength. She'd relied on it, and needed it with a desperation that consumed her and caused her head to fall gently against his chest, resting there for just for a moment.

"One dance with the girl who knows my every move," he whispered. "That's all I'm asking for."

One last dance, she told herself.

Laney breathed in his scent, yummy male with a punch of high-octane testosterone, and a sweetness that was addictive. The last time he held her like this, she'd finally found the courage to leave Simon. Rhett had given her a safe place to stay, a shoulder to cry on, and promised her everything would work out.

In a way, it had. Simon was a nightmare of her past. She was growing stronger every day, and knew that there were good men out there. Men who admired strength in a woman, and didn't try to snuff it out.

And it was that strength that she would rely on to get her through the next few moments—and the next few months.

"I don't feel much like dancing, Rhett," she said, stepping back. "I just came to tell you how happy I am for you, and that you deserve every ounce of love that comes your way. You're a good man."

He studied her long and hard, until she felt the tears she'd been holding back start to surface.

"What's going on?" He cupped her cheek. "You look pale. Is it another migraine?"

His hand felt smooth and comforting against her cheek, while the calluses on his musician's fingers made tiny shivers scatter across her bare skin. She swallowed several times before she spoke, praying she wouldn't sound as choked up as she felt. "It's not my head that aches."

She couldn't feel anything over the aching in her heart. Rhett's genuine concern served as a reminder of how much she was losing. No one cared for her like he had, and now that he was getting married, taking care of her would be inappropriate.

The weeks that followed the announcement of his engagement dragged by and her grief had turned to a dull longing. Hanging in the background of her every breath was the constant reminder of the changes that would come. And losing Rhett wasn't the only change headed her way.

Gone would be the closeness they shared, the comfortable silent moments, and the pee-your-pants laughing ones. The ones that were so intense no words were needed to express the awesomeness of it.

Now, a ring was in play. In less than twenty-four hours, vows were to be exchanged, and this had to be goodbye.

"I hate to cut out early, but I can't do this right now," she said.

His familiar face, overflowing with concern, loomed over her and made the ache even worse. "Okay. Let's grab a seat and I'll get you a drink."

He slid his palms down her bare arms and grasped her hands, offering comfort and understanding, but he didn't understand, and all of the sudden it became imperative that he did.

"Not the dancing, Rhett. *This.*" She gestured back and forth between them to encompass the enormity of her words. "I can't do this right now...I have to go." Her voice broke on the last word.

"Whoa, don't cry. Give me a minute and I'll just grab Gage's keys and give you a ride home."

"You can't leave," she said, horrified. "It's *your* rehearsal dinner."

"But driving at night is bad for a migraine."

And staying here for one more moment would be bad for her heart. The weight of her decision was all-consuming. Her chest tightened to the point of agony and the bile that had been churning in her stomach for the past six weeks burned the back of her throat.

She didn't have any destination in mind. Only knew she had to get out. Spread her wings and find her own happiness—so that Rhett could hold on to his.

"I'll be fine." She'd weathered storms rougher than this. "Be happy, Rhett."

With one last glance, to put every nuance of his face to memory, Laney turned to walk through the rose garden, the pungent fragrance stinging her nose, the weight of the night clinging to her skin. And when she was out of sight, she did what she'd always done—she ran.

Out of Rhett's life and away from the only home she had ever known.

About the Author

Marina Adair is a #1 National best-selling author and holds a Master of Fine arts in creative writing. Along with the Eastons series, she is also the author the St. Helena Vineyard series, the Heroes of St Helena series, and her upcoming Sequoia Lake series. She currently lives with her husband, daughter, and two neurotic cats in Northern California.

As a writer, Marina is devoted to giving her readers contemporary romance where the towns are small, the personalities large, and the romance explosive. She also loves to interact with readers and you can catch her on Facebook or visit her at www.MarinaAdair.com. Keep up with Marina by signing up for her newsletter at www.MarinaAdair.com/newsletter.

Sign Me Up!